More praise for Missing Persons

Stephanie Carpenter's protagonists are mostly from socio-economic backgrounds that teach them the need to brace themselves for what's to come, and while they want to believe that things aren't as bad with their loved ones present, they're also aware that they have no way of knowing. These stories are piercingly smart on how unsettling our everyday intimacies can be, and heartening in their faith in our responsibility to always make sure that we've nevertheless done what we could.
    —Jim Shepard, author of *The Book of Aron* and *The World to Come*

Sometimes what's missing is best unfound. *Missing Persons*, the remarkable debut story collection by Stephanie Carpenter, illuminates the loss of a father due to mental illness, an aloof living statue, a city that takes things away, a 19th century philanderer who doesn't recognize his lost daughter, not to mention a giant poodle named Saucepan. The aching feminism of "Trial Watchers" vies with the sorry history of a lover's dead mother in "Inheritance." Always mellifluous, Carpenter has an Alice Munro facility to "embed more than announce." But here's the announcement: *Missing Persons* achieves a deep and timely look into the void.
    —Terese Svoboda, author of *Anything That Burns You: A Portrait of Lola Ridge, Radical Poet*

An urban angel. A Victorian philanderer. A dystopian word game with murky origins. An online dating relationship gone horribly wrong. These sharp, distinctive stories hit the sweet spot between realism and allegory. Readers will be won over by Carpenter's dry wit and the almost mathematical precision of her language, tools she employs, with great artistry, to unearth surprising emotional states.
    —Trudy Lewis, author of *The Empire Rolls*

Stephanie Carpenter's stories display a wealth of quirky characters, difficult situations of their own making, and astonishing falls from grace, related with meticulous prose and an eye for the telling detail. Endings surprise without gimmicks, dialogue manages to be simultaneously sharp and awkward, and the results satisfy and trouble us in equal measure. *Missing Persons* marks the beginning of an exciting career.

—Thomas C. Foster, author of *How to Read Literature Like a Professor*

Missing Persons

missing persons

Winner of the 2017 Press 53 Award for Short Fiction

Stephanie Carpenter

Press 53
Winston-Salem

Press 53, LLC
PO Box 30314
Winston-Salem, NC 27130

First Edition

Cover design by Éireann Lorsung
ohbara.com

Author photo by Adam Johnson
brockit inc.

Library of Congress Control Number 2017954773

Printed on acid-free paper
ISBN 978-1-941209-63-9

For Andy and Lars, who are missed.

The author offers grateful thanks to the editors of the following publications where the stories listed below first appeared:

Avery: An Anthology of New Fiction, Vol. 5, "Apnea"

Big Fiction, No. 2, "Mr. Codman's Women"

Crab Orchard Review, Vol. 13, No. 2, "Witnesses"

LITnIMAGE, No. 14, "Lost Boy Not Found"

The Missouri Review, Vol. 40, No. 3, "The Longest Night of the Year"

Nimrod International Journal, Vol. 59, No. 1, "The Sweeper"

Quiddity International Literary Journal, Vol. 8, No. 1, "The Mission"

The Saint Ann's Review, Vol. 6, No. 1, "Inheritance"

turnrow, Vol. 6, No. 1, "Living Statues"

Witness, Vol. 29, No. 1, "Trial Watchers"

contents

witnesses

The ceiling is lit red and blue when Jacob wakes up. He crawls to the end of his bed, lifts the corner of the window curtain. A squad car is parked across the way, next to the convenience store at the crossroads. Jacob can see a huddle of men out front, beside the big white ice chest, and inside the store, a beam of light flashing across the coolers. Then a German Shepherd slinks out, pulling its handler. The dog casts about for a scent; the officer jerks on its choke chain. Jacob sees the dog raise its nose as it turns in small circles. It sniffs the still air, then points its muzzle toward the trailer. The officer lifts his flashlight, and Jacob ducks, quickly.

"Go back to sleep," his mother murmurs. The corner of her eye mask has shifted to one side.

"I was thirsty," he says. "I just wanted a drink, is all."

"Sure," she says. "Sleep."

"There's cops out there."

"That's good. Shhh."

"Fine," he says. "Good*night.*"

She doesn't respond, and he knows that she has already fallen asleep.

Jacob tiptoes past the foot of his mother's bed and pushes open the bedroom door. It is darker in the kitchen, the digital displays of the microwave and coffee maker like signposts. And also like decoys. He waits for his pupils to dilate, then moves around the breakfast bar, low and quick. He crouches beside the front door. Whoever brought the police to the store is probably somewhere outside—maybe close by. In the crawl space beneath their trailer. In the middle of the fat lilac bush. His hand rests on the deadbolt. If something were to happen—to him—he would have time to make some sort of noise. *Police. A dog.* He is sure of it. He turns the bolt, drags the door open just slightly. He can't see the men from here or even make out the road very clearly. But if he opens the screen door, someone might hear—if not his mother, then one of the criminals. If he sneaks outside, he will surely get caught. He presses slowly on the door latch.

"All right," one of the men calls. "We'll let you know." An engine turns over; the police siren bleats briefly. Jacob touches his foot to the stabbing green blades of the doormat.

"Jacob." His mother is behind him, with her eye mask pushed all the way back. "I don't think so."

"I thought I heard something." He steps back inside. "I was just checking."

"That's fine." She nudges him aside, relocks the doors. "Leave it to me. I want you back in bed by the time I count to ten. One…"

"Mom," he says. "I'll go back to bed."

"So go," she says. "Two . . ."

"I'm getting some water first. Is it okay if I get some water?"

"Show me how fast you can pour water. I'm at five."

"Forget it," he says. She waits for him to pass her. On opposite sides of the Chinese screen, they climb back into their beds.

"Goodnight, Jake." Soon his mother is breathing evenly. But Jacob knows he's done for the night. He lies on his back and stares at the blank ceiling. The colored lights are gone now, but he is still jittery. He is a bad sleeper, jittery often; most nights he is still awake at midnight when the convenience store closes and the bedroom darkens fully. His mother sleeps soundly while he lies on his back and listens to the trees out behind the trailer—their noises faint but heart-stopping even from this, the front bedroom. A broken stick, a crying bird. The trees end at the river, and beyond the river stretches unbroken state land. He thinks of predatory animals, moving low to the ground. He thinks of pale deer at the edge of their lawn, and behind the deer, driving them forward, the kind of men who live in the woods. Survivalists. He has read *My Side of the Mountain*; he has seen segments on the news about an Indian woman who lives year-round at the State Park. People can still live on nuts and berries. His father could start a fire with two sticks, and set a snare. His father could live off the land, if he had to. If it came to that.

It is five the last time he remembers checking his luminescent watch, and then it is six, and his mother's alarm wakes him up again.

This is the first summer Jacob has been allowed to stay by himself. His mother gets back from work in the late afternoon; the boys who live up the road race four-wheelers all day. He used to be friends with them in the summer, no matter what happened at school. But they're older, and rougher, and it is as though they have forgotten his name. So Jacob reads a lot of books. He watches a lot of TV. And he goes to the convenience store every day, whether or not he needs anything.

He sees no sign of the break-in when he enters that afternoon. Walt—the owner—stands behind the counter, with the sports page spread in front of him. He's older than Jacob's mother, a bearish man with a bald spot, who smokes in the store.

He stubs out a cigarette when he sees Jacob. "Destry rides again!"

"I guess." Jacob skirts the potato chip rack and heads to the grocery coolers. They're always the same—loudly humming and poorly stocked—but he takes his time anyway.

When he brings his drink to the register there is another person in line, a girl a few inches taller than he is. She's redeeming a trash bag full of pop cans.

"Those better not be all full of butts and sand," Walt says.

"I don't know." She rests one foot on the newspaper rack below the counter. She has a black toenail, about to fall off.

"Where'd you pick them up? I don't want some sandy cans dug out of the garbage."

"What's it matter? You have to give me the money. That's the law."

Walt shakes his head. "Did you pay for all of these? Because otherwise, that's fraudulent redemption."

The girl glances back at Jacob. "Come *on*," she whispers.

"This one time." Walt begins counting the empties through the plastic bag. "Four dollars and thirty cents." He slides the money across the counter. "And that's it. You start buying stuff in here, I'll take your cans. Otherwise, don't let me see you back."

The girl grabs the bills, scattering the coins to the tile floor. By the time Jacob has picked them up, she's gone.

"Don't ever let me see you doing that," Walt tells him. "Did you see what that looked like? A bum."

Jacob nods. The window behind the register, he notices, is cracked in a sunburst pattern. Beneath it stretch long shelves of liquor.

"I saw the police last night," Jacob says.

"Well, maybe this time they'll catch them," says Walt. "But I'm not holding my breath." He rings up Jacob's strawberry milk. "You have a good one, kid."

When Jacob steps outside, into the hot, bright sunlight, the girl is still in the parking lot, leaning on the hood of Walt's car. She smiles when she sees him.

"Hey," she says. "You're Jacob, right?"

He nods. Face to face, he recognizes her, too, as the younger sister of his former babysitter. Like Cheryl, his babysitter, the girl has long sandy hair and a thin, pale face. She is older than him by several years.

"Are you going home?"

He shakes his milk. "I guess."

She nods her head. "I'm Shauna. Can you have people over?"

"Not usually."

"You live right there, right? I live over there." She points down the south arm of the T intersection. A cluster of houses is just visible, past the mechanic's shop and behind the Assembly of Christ church; he knows that her family lives in one of these. "You know Cheryl, right? So is it all right if I come over?"

"Why?"

She squints at him. "You have TV, don't you?"

"Yeah, but not cable."

"Well, that's good enough."

"What's wrong with your TV?"

"We can't have one anymore," she says. "You *know*." She gestures again, down the road, toward the white clapboard church. Then he does know—or remember, really: that spring, their pastor had ordered them all to get rid of their TVs and radios. There'd been piles out with the trash. *He'll tell them to stop reading next,* Jacob's mother had said. *The man is crazy.* Jacob's father had belonged to that church, the Assembly of Christ.

"So can I?"

Jacob considers the long hours ahead of him, the tedium. What his mother might say. But Shauna is only one person; what could be the harm? "I guess."

"Thank God." She follows him across the road and he opens the front door with his latchkey. The living room, wood-paneled, seems especially dark after the sunlight, but he is glad he keeps things neat.

Shauna kicks off her flip-flops next to the door. "Who lives here?"

"Me and my mom. We used to have a renter but she moved out."

"God, I am so glad to see this." She drops onto the middle cushion of the couch and picks up the remote. "You have no idea."

Jacob watches as she flips through the channels. She finds her soap opera and settles back. It's nothing he wants to watch: pointless conversation against fake-looking backdrops. But he doesn't complain. When it's over she sighs and turns to him.

"You're so lucky," she says. "Is it okay if I come over every day?"

"I don't know," he says. "I mean, I'll have to ask."

She rolls her eyes. "Just as long as your mom doesn't call my mom or anything, okay? Because this is exactly what I'm not supposed to be doing right now. God, it's the worst." She picks at her dead toenail. "Where is your mom, anyway?"

"At work."

"Well, yeah. But *where* is what I mean."

"She works in town."

"Doing what?"

"She works for a hotline? For women?" He can feel himself flushing.

Shauna's eyes widen. "Like phone sex?"

He shakes his head. "*No.* Like if women are in trouble, with their boyfriends or whatever . . . you know."

She is staring at him. "You mean abortions?"

His heart beats—fast. "It's not just that. It's for people who are in trouble."

She sits up a little bit. "God."

"You can't tell your parents," he says. "Seriously."

"Okay." But she is looking around as though the room has changed all of a sudden.

"How come you can't have TV?" Jacob asks loudly. His is not the only strange family; he wants her to see this.

She shakes herself a little. "How come? I don't know. Because we're too worldly. That's what pastor said. I don't know."

"That's stupid," he says. "What do you do instead?"

"Nothing. Read religious stuff. I don't know. Nothing. I'm about sick of it, believe me. And next year I'm supposed to get home-schooled. Pastor says it's a blessing the buses got cut." She picks at the toenail again. "What about you? What are you doing next year?"

"I'm going into town. Since my mom drives in anyway."

"That's cool." Shauna takes a long drink from the Coke he served her. "My dad says they don't have time to drive me even over to Regional. Maybe I could get a ride with you?"

He shrugs. "My mom's driving me to the junior high. So I don't know."

"That's cool," she says. "I'm in ninth next year."

"You're in *ninth*?" He had thought tenth, at least.

"What? Like you're so smart."

"I get A's."

"In *elementary* school. You think that means something? That doesn't mean *anything*."

"No," he says. "In *seventh* grade. I made the honor roll."
He shrugs. "I'll ask my mom about it."

"Fine," she says. "It's only until I get my license, anyway.
I mean, even if I have to stay home, it's only a year or
something, right?" She tugs at the ends of her hair. "I'm
not even sure my dad would let me ride with you. With
your mom and all. I mean, no offense."

They sit on the couch in silence. Another soap opera
has started, worse than the first one. Shauna flips the
channels, then turns off the set.

"I'll see you tomorrow," she says. "All right?"

After Shauna leaves Jacob cleans up after her, draining their
pop cans in the sink: two instead of one. His mother might
wonder about that. If Shauna comes again, he won't have
one. He arranges the pillows and afghan on the couch like
usual and turns the channel back to the one he likes, a food
channel that sometimes comes in cleanly if he's careful with
the antennae. He has only read twenty pages; if his mother
asks, he'll claim a headache. He will not, he realizes, tell her
that anyone has been there. At best, she would ask
questions; at worst, she would say it had to stop.

In the evenings, he and his mother eat dinner, watch
reality shows, page restlessly through their books. Jacob can
never mark the exact moment he begins worrying that he
won't sleep, but always, by the time he goes to bed, he's
been thinking about it for a while. Once in the middle of a
very bad stretch his mother had given him one of her pills,
but though they'd cut it in half, it had still seemed like too
much, to him: the feeling of something alien pulling him
away into unconsciousness. Every time it started to work,
he had jerked, like he was falling in a dream, until finally he
lay in bed in a sweat. They'd tried other things, too: warm
milk, useless, viscous; night-time cough syrups that made

him hear things—as though people were talking in the next room. So now he lies awake and waits, or sends his mind out searching. For the best friend who moved away in second grade. For the time they went to Chicago for Thanksgiving. And, inevitably, for his father. There's only so much Jacob can remember. Once, he held his father's hand, walking across a hospital parking lot. His grandmother had been there, too. Jacob had been terrified of the wide sewer grates in the lot—the adults had swung him across. Did they go inside the hospital that day? He can't remember who they were visiting; he can only remember his grandmother's face from pictures. But he can see his father, on that day, just as he can see him coming home at night—a dark-haired man in a mechanic's jumpsuit. On Sundays his father would give Jacob quarters for the collection plate; he would sing all the church songs from memory. And Jacob can remember, once, going with his father to watch a fire. The bar that had burned that day was rebuilt, immediately. It's only a few miles away, near the highway, and Jacob knows now that women dance there topless. Then, he hadn't known much. The day the bar burned, Jacob had stood in the parking lot with his father, watching the fire department trying to control the flames. They were volunteer firemen, with a small yellow truck instead of the long red engine that, as a little boy, he'd so loved. He had seen as well as anyone that they would not save the building. The pastor had been in the parking lot, too, on that day; he'd clapped Jacob's father on the back, and they had both repeated, God's will be done. Nobody had tried to get Jacob to say this; he'd said it of his own volition, to his mother, when they got home. They'd walked in smelling like smoke, and he'd said to her, the bar burned down, God's will be done. He could remember the look on her face, like the time he'd dislocated his arm. That's all Jacob can remember from that day.

When Jacob can't sleep, he pictures his father, living in the woods or in vacant buildings. His father might be in a homeless shelter somewhere, or in a state home. Jacob never imagines that his father has gone on to better things. When he tries to invent such a story, it falls apart quickly. His father can't be working under his own name, or the government would catch him for desertion, for child support. It seems unlikely that he could have invented a functional new identity. The only better place he might be is Heaven, and Jacob does pray for this, and he tries hard to mean it.

In the morning the police are there again, standing beneath Walt's cracked window, two men writing on notepads. Jacob could give them names; anyone nearby could name the five people most likely to have done it. But of course that's not enough, that's only speculation. For the moment there's a ring of safety extending from the cops around the store— and almost to Jacob. When they leave it will be gone. The police station is fifteen miles away. The fire station is farther.

Shauna arrives right before her show begins. Jacob tries to keep reading, but it's hard to concentrate with the TV turned up high and Shauna beside him, winding her long hair again and again around her finger. It doesn't smell fruity, like most girls' hair, but minty instead. Her legs, propped on the coffee table, are pale and stubbled.

"That's John," she says. She thinks he is watching the show. "That same actor used to play Roman, but then the old Roman came back, and it turned out that John was some other guy that had been brainwashed into impersonating Roman. And that's Marlena." Marlena's face is still and sorrowing; John's is lifeless against white pillows. They hold this pose until a commercial starts. "For a while it seemed like she was a serial killer but actually this evil wizard had just imprisoned everybody on a desert island."

"Sure." Jacob holds up the book he's been reading: *Robinson Crusoe*. On the cover, Crusoe points sternly at a tropical bird.

"I've heard of this." She takes it from him, turning it in her hands. "'Young Reader's Christian Library.'" This is the name of the publisher.

He shrugs. "It's the only copy they had at the library."

"Do you like this kind of stuff?" She looks at him. "I mean, no offense, but you're not a Christian, right?"

His face is burning. "Why not?"

"I don't know—do you even believe in God?"

He believes that something is watching him all the time, something that he can neither appease nor evade. "Do you?"

"Of course." She sighs. "I mean, I know that God has a plan for us and everything. But sometimes—I mean, what's the difference between reading this and watching TV?"

"Nothing?" Jacob thinks of his father; he takes a deep breath. "Did you ever think—maybe *you're* the one being brainwashed?"

She laughs. "Like TV's really that bad. As long as you've got good values, who cares?"

Jacob shrugs: she has missed his point entirely. "Maybe you should ask your pastor."

"It just gets frustrating sometimes." She tosses the book into his lap. "But for real, you should come with me next Sunday. I mean, if you want." She turns the volume back up. "Pastor welcomes new people."

Jacob finds his place in *Robinson Crusoe*. He wouldn't go to their church if it were the last place on earth.

The days and nights move on and on, until Jacob's routine has expanded to include soap operas. Then comes a day of the sort he dreads: the sky close, the air hot and vacuum-tight. Tornado weather. It might have been centuries since one touched down in their town—it certainly hasn't happened in his memory, or his mother's. But he has seen the kind of homes most often featured in television news stories. If a tornado comes, it is coming for their trailer. And what would he do? He watches the warnings scroll across the bottom of the TV screen, for counties south of theirs. The blocked-off counties turn from green to red in the weatherman's map. Finally Jacob steps outside, into the heavy air. At the crossroads, just a couple hundred yards away, he will be able to see far in every direction. He lowers his head, begins to run, and when he gets there, he stops only briefly, seeing nothing, before wheeling and sprinting back. There is no one around to jeer at him for running badly. Nobody is racing four-wheelers. The birds are quiet. The sky is yellowish, greenish, and he is sweating heavily. He stumbles up the three steps to the door.

"Boo!" someone cries—from inside the trailer. Jacob yells, jumping back into the porch railing. Someone inside—he didn't lock up! He didn't lock the door behind him, when the store has just been burgled, and down the road, people come and go all night from the old farmhouses. It is not safe, not safe, not safe—

"*Jacob*," says the intruder. "I got you, didn't I?" A face comes into view on the other side of the dark screen: Shauna. She opens the door to him. "Were you scared?"

"You shouldn't just barge into people's houses," he says. "It's against the law to trespass. And it's bad manners."

She sighs. "But it's time for *Days*."

He pushes past her. His chest is tight; he leans on the breakfast bar for a moment before getting her a Coke.

They settle into the couch. Jacob decides to watch the show, to distract himself from the warnings. An hourglass fills the television screen. He rests his head on a throw pillow, curls his legs on the couch cushion. It seems as though he has heard these vague conversations before. The characters wear party clothes in the daytime; they repeat themselves mindlessly: Salem, Stefano, helicopters . . . for once, he can't stay awake.

"Jacob." He opens his eyes when Shauna begins shaking him. The theme song of the next soap opera is playing.

"Jacob, I'm just going to go, all right? I'll see you, okay?"

The map in the corner of the television screen has turned wholly red.

"Can I come with you?" he says. "*Please.*"

She shakes her head. "My mom has daycare. I can't have people over."

He points to the map. "It's an emergency."

She looks at the TV screen, then back at him. "You're scared of *that*? My Gran was in a tornado once, in Florida. It hit everybody else's trailer but hers." She bites her lip. "Oh, fine—come on."

Jacob gets his emergency backpack from beneath his bed and locks the door behind them. They hurry through the crossroads, to the Assembly of Christ and just beyond.

Shauna stops him at the foot of her driveway. The yard is enclosed in chain-link and scattered with squat plastic toys. The house is a small white ranch.

"My mom might be kind of pissed about this," she says. "So don't take it personal, okay?"

He nods. His mother would be pissed, too—at him for going inside such a place. They are cultish, she says. They have a mob mentality.

He follows Shauna to the door, on the other side of which several Yorkies are barking deliriously. "Shauna!" yells a far-off voice, as soon as the door opens. "Shauna, that had better be you!"

"Come on." She leads him through the living room, where the furniture is still arranged around the missing television. A set of steep stairs lead down from the kitchen. At the bottom is an open room, evidently the daycare. Cheryl, his old babysitter, sits folded into a child's-sized plastic chair, while a handful of little kids play with large blocks on the tile floor around her. Sliding glass doors give way to the backyard. The basement is barely below-ground at all.

"What's *he* doing here?" Cheryl doesn't smile at Jacob or stand.

"I'm witnessing to him." Shauna glances quickly at Jacob and he shrugs.

Cheryl looks at Jacob, and it isn't that she's forgotten him. They had gone on nature walks together, the summer that he was eleven. They had pressed flowers in old books and killed beetles for his collection using nail polish remover. But her expression says something different. "I'm telling Mom you been gone again."

"Oh, what's the difference?" Shauna says. "She'll be mad at me anyways." She takes Jacob's hand in both of hers; her palms are dry and smooth. "Have you accepted Jesus as your personal savior?" She makes her voice sweet and earnest. "Why don't you come with me and I'll tell you all about Him." Jacob can feel heat moving up his body; she does not release his hands.

"Shauna—" Cheryl begins.

"We'll be in the boys' room." Shauna pulls Jacob after her through the mess of toys and toddling kids. At the far end of the basement is a pressboard door. She throws it open so that it reaches the full width of its hinges and bounces back at them.

The bedroom on the other side is cool and dim, with just a small window set high on the back wall. A young man with a closely trimmed beard sits on the edge of a twin bed. He wears a large cross on a leather cord about his neck; he holds a guitar upside down. Despite the noise of their entry, he does not seem startled. He looks up at them and smiles.

"What are you doing home?" Shauna says. "Travis, what are you doing here?"

The young man plays a series of chords. In contrast to Shauna, he seems very, very calm. "And who is this?" He looks up at Jacob.

"Jacob, my brother Travis; Travis, Jacob. Aren't you supposed to be at work, Travis?"

Travis closes his eyes and begins to sing. "*We waste those hours we don't praise you / we waste those days when we don't pray/ If we sing your glory, might we raise you? / oh Lord, speed me to that da-ay.*" He blinks. "I've been working on that one since dawn."

"That's great," Shauna says flatly. She drops to her knees and rummages beneath the second twin bed. "Do you like Sorry!?" she asks Jacob. "We had to get rid of everything else."

"It's like God sent me this song to share with you," Travis says.

"Sit down," Shauna tells Jacob, and he joins her cross-legged on the linoleum floor. She shuffles the playing cards roughly. "Why aren't you at work, Travis?"

"I've been full of it all day," Travis says. "God's glory, you know? Jacob, I'm sure *you* know: I have loved Jacob— that's Genesis, man. You're the beloved, you know?"

"I'm blue," says Shauna. She sets up green for Jacob. "Travis, are you playing or what?"

He laughs and starts strumming chords. He uses the fingers of his right hand on the fretboard, those of his left hand to strike the strings.

Jacob can't stop watching these bizarre, backwards movements. "Why do you hold it wrong?"

Travis chuckles. "Well, I busted up my hand pretty good when I was your age, Jacob, and after it healed, I couldn't play anymore. So I learned to play left-handed instead. Good as ever." He smiles, and there is something familiar about him, to Jacob—the shininess of the smile, the unyielding directness of his gaze.

"How'd you break your hand?" Jacob asks. He knows it's a prying question.

"I punched a brick wall," says Travis. "I was full of hate back then, you know? And when I'd get angry, Jacob, all I wanted to do was use my fists. But then God blessed me with that accident, and afterward, He showed me how to use my hands in prayer, instead. And in glorifying Him through music." Travis smiles, strumming. "Yes, I was born at the age of thirteen, my friend."

Shauna draws a card and moves her pawn. "It's your *turn*," she tells Jacob. "Travis, I think you're late for work."

He laughs. "I'm doing other work today, my sister."

Jacob moves his pawn. Through the small window, the sky still looks green. He wonders how long he'll have to wait here. He wonders whether they'd let him call his mom.

"Jacob I have loved, but Esau I have hated," says Travis. "Jacob, man, you've got to get with it."

"Travis, shut *up*." Shauna bumps one of Jacob's green pawns back to Start. "Sorry."

"Could we turn on the radio?" asks Jacob. "To hear about the tornado?"

"No," says Shauna. "No radio, no TV, no decent music."

"Jacob," says Travis, "why haven't we seen you at Youth Ministry?"

"Tell him why *you're* not there anymore, Travis," says Shauna. "Why don't you tell him about that?"

"How are we going to know if it's coming?" asks Jacob. "How do you guys know what's going on?"

Travis begins laughing, lying back on the bed with the guitar across his chest. "We know, we know," he says. "Trust Him to give you peace in your storm."

"He wouldn't leave this girl alone," Shauna says. "He wouldn't stop calling a *fifteen-year-old girl.* How old does he look to you, Jacob?"

"I should go," says Jacob. It's 3:30 by the clock on the nightstand. "I should get home before my mom does. Or she'll worry."

"What about the tornado?" Shauna is staring at him. "I thought you were so scared."

"It'll be fine." But that patch of sky still looks fearsome.

"I'm so sure you'll be fine in your trailer," she says. "You just don't want to lose."

"Where do you live, little brother? I'll drive you home." Travis sits up and smiles again at Jacob.

"He lives by that convenience store you've been praying on," says Shauna.

"Not in David Trenor's old place?" Travis frowns.

"That's his dad, you retard." Shauna sweeps the Sorry! cards and pawns back into their box.

"Your father was a holy man, Jacob." Travis shakes his head. "He's in my prayers still. And you are, too, even though I didn't know who you were. Let them know You, Lord, that's what I've prayed."

"You know you can't go anywhere with the car while all those babies are here," Shauna says. "You know that, right Travis? Because something could happen at literally any moment."

"What are you praying about the store?" Jacob thinks of the liquor, the cigarettes.

"The usual," Shauna says. "God's judgment."

Travis is still watching Jacob. "Do you know Him?"

Jacob shrugs.

"Jacob, do you know the Good News?" Travis leans forward.

"People who don't go to your church can still read the Bible," says Jacob.

"If you're going, why don't you go?" Shauna says.

"Tell me about the Bible, Jacob," says Travis. "Faith comes by hearing, and hearing by the word of God."

"I like the Revelation," says Jacob. "I like the part about the exodus from Egypt. Exodus, I guess that is."

"There we go." Travis leans back. "There we go." He plays a scale on his guitar. "No man shall see me and live."

"What the hell, Travis," says Shauna.

"Shauna!" yells a woman. "Shauna, get up here right now!"

"No need to leave, Jake," says Travis. "Let's rap some more. Share the Good Word."

"Come *on*." Shauna pulls Jacob to his feet. She is stronger than he is, he can feel it in her hands. Their fronts brush together briefly and she rolls her eyes. Once they're in the empty daycare, she pushes him toward the glass doors. "Just go home." The Yorkies bark around their ankles, darting in and out of the house. "Just—I'll see you later, okay?" And she slams the door, twists the lock.

Jacob runs through the choking air and because the sky is still green, and their house still a trailer, he waits with Walt in the store until he sees his mother's car pull into the drive.

The next day is Saturday—no soap operas—and he knows that Shauna will not come. Nor is she likely to come on Sunday, when, he remembers dimly, there are several long sermons in the clapboard church, with Sunday school in between. He was six the last time he sat through it, but he hasn't quite forgotten the misery of a full day spent in the hot church, or of his father's hand, sharp on his knee, if he gave way to the urge to kick the Bible rack, or draw on a collection envelope. Now, he and his mother sometimes go to a Lutheran church in town, where the service lasts exactly an hour. He might get confirmed there, if they're willing to baptize him first.

Jacob's mother takes him swimming on Saturday at Torch Lake, to the narrow public beach in the midst of the resorts. It's one of the ten most beautiful lakes in the world, according to *National Geographic,* and deep like Loch Ness or Lake Champlain. They don't have a monster, though—the water is clear all the way to the bottom—but in the middle of the lake, in its cold, cold depths, is a pleasure party that went through the ice, back in the days of horses and carriages. Frozen as if they'd died on the Russian steppe, in their queer old clothes, with their hair lifted up by the water. Jacob has never been boating on this lake, has never looked down. To think about it from shore is more than enough.

Jacob and his mother get ice cream cones after they've swum; they stop at the library so he can stock up for the week. Later, back home, his mother stands at the kitchen sink, snapping beans for dinner, and he sits at the breakfast bar, leafing through his books.

"Jacob," she says. "What if we spent some time tomorrow fixing up the other room for you?"

He stops twisting on his barstool. "What about getting another renter?"

"Harriet isn't coming back." His mother turns from the sink to face him across the bar. "I'd let somebody else come here if they needed to, but I'd prefer—and I'm sure you would, too—to have a little more room."

"But we need the money, right? Maybe we should put an ad in the paper or something. Or I could make signs and hang them up."

"Jacob, don't worry about it. I'm saying it's fine. And my guess is you'll sleep better by yourself—don't you think?"

He thinks—of the woods, the drug houses, the Assembly of Christ, praying against the convenience store. Of what she earns every week, divided by the two of them and multiplied by everything they need or will need. She can sleep through all of that, and more.

"You'll love it, I promise." His mother smiles at him. "We'll get started tomorrow. Read to me a little, would you, while I'm cooking?"

He opens the topmost book, *The Light in the Forest*: "'The boy was about fifteen years old,'" he reads. "'He tried to stand very straight and tall when he heard the news, but inside of him everything had gone black.'"

His mother raises her eyebrows but continues snapping beans.

Monday Shauna does not come, and Jacob falls back into his routine, visiting the store, reading and rereading his books. He plays solitaire with cards that have begun to soften around the edges; he weeds their small garden several times a day. If he were braver he might hike back on the state land, looking for blackberries, or interesting bugs. But even on Tuesday he can't force himself to go beyond viewing distance of the trailer. He is encircled by noises whenever he enters the woods, and every flash of color in the trees is one of the rough teenagers from down the street, or a survivalist, stalking him. Wednesday passes; there is a month and a half left of vacation. He lies awake at night and sits, stunned, during the days.

But on Thursday, Shauna is back. Jacob is watching a cooking show when he hears her, running her nails softly over the screen.

"I had to help out at the daycare," she tells him. "Cheryl raised hell. She's supposed to be studying for her GEDs and instead Mom's had her taking care of babies. I can just see what next year's going to be like for me." She flops onto the couch. "Hey—did your mom say whether she could drive me in to school?"

He feels his face redden. "Not yet," he says.

She watches him. "She doesn't know if she can yet, or you didn't ask her?"

"There's a lot of paperwork," he says. "It's not like you can just show up in another school district and nobody cares."

"But what did she say?" asks Shauna. "Whatever—you didn't ask. Maybe I should call her at that hotline and ask myself?"

"You don't even know her name."

"Yeah? Her name's Janet Trenor. Her *Redbooks* are all over the place, in case you haven't noticed."

"She doesn't use her *real* name on the phone."

"Maybe not, but I bet I could convince them to let me talk to her. If I told them how her dear son had broken his arm and was on his way to the emergency room."

"Just don't, okay? I'll ask her later."

"Fine." Shauna sets her bare feet on the coffee table. Her black toenail, he sees, has finally fallen off. Where a nail should be, the skin is shiny and dark pink. "You know, pastor prayed for your dad at meeting last night."

For a second he has to close his eyes, against the toe, the pastor. *Inside of him everything had gone black.*

"I don't understand how come everybody carries on about him." Shauna looks at Jacob. "I mean, it was a long time ago."

Jacob nods, slowly. "I was six."

"And it's not like he's not the only man in this shit town that's run off on his wife."

He stares at the TV, at a sharp knife, cleaving a tomato. "No," he agrees.

"Then why not let it drop? I mean, what's the big deal?"

"You should ask your pastor." He can hear the meanness in his voice. "See what he says."

"Come *on*—just tell me." She bounces a little on the couch cushion.

"It was all his fault." He finds that he can't say any more.

"I'm so sure," Shauna says. But she looks confused.

Jacob closes his eyes again. "My dad was sick—I don't remember, but he was. He was on medicine. But your pastor told him not to take it—because of God. So my dad stopped. And then I don't really know. Then he left."

"We *go* to the doctor," Shauna says. "We're not freaks."

Jacob turns the channel to the familiar daytime commercials that flank her show. He throws the remote on the coffee table. "Not that kind of doctor." He sighs. "A psychiatrist."

"Oh." She watches the TV screen. "Well. So what, then—he was crazy?"

"*No*," says Jacob. "He had an illness. Or has one."

"But, then—are *you* okay? I mean, how does it work with that kind of thing?" She shakes her head. "I've never known anyone who—had that kind of illness."

He shrugs. "It's not like you can always tell."

Shauna bites her lip. She lays her hand on his shoulder. "I'm sorry."

He shrugs again. "It's better than you thinking he just ran away from us." Though sometimes, truthfully, this is what Jacob would prefer to think. That his father is not starving, or lost, or dead—but that he ran away from this life: the pastor, the wife, the kid, the expenses. That he made a choice. "Here," Jacob says. "I'll get his picture."

He goes to his bedroom—his new bedroom, at the back of the trailer, ablaze with sunlight at this time of day—and pulls his emergency backpack from under his bed. There are fruit roll-ups and iodine tablets, fishing line, gauze, and in a thick envelope, a copy of their last church portrait. He carries it in to her. It has been a long time since he's looked at it.

Shauna draws the portrait from the envelope. In front of a blue-gray screen, Jacob's family poses in nice outfits: his mother younger and prettier, Jacob with a bowl-cut, and his father, leaning forward slightly, thin, dark, the apex of their small triangle. What might he have been thinking in this moment, under the photographer's lights, with the two of them sitting there in front of him? A month later he was gone, and the two halves of his father's face look to Jacob now like a creation in a little kid's flip book, where Groucho glasses might be paired with a Cheshire grin. The mouth is smiling, but that smile seems as though it could turn at any minute, into a new expression, to match the staring, strange eyes.

"We get this same backdrop," Shauna says. "Every time." She holds the photo carefully by its edges. "You were cute."

"Yeah, well." He rubs his eyes.

"My brother wanted me to say that you were welcome to come by and see him whenever."

Jacob looks at his father, at his own younger self. He does not want to see Travis again.

"I'll pray for him," she says. "Your dad. If that's okay."

He slips the photograph back between sheets of tissue paper, back into its heavy envelope. How could a prayer be anything but good? "Thanks." Then he notices the hourglass on the television screen. "Oh—hey, it's time."

He turns up the volume, and already the storylines are becoming clearer to him: a bunch of people, in a made-up place, whose lives seem not to change from day to day. Theirs is a world where, as Shauna has explained to him, someone might disappear for months or years, given up for dead, and then force his way back into the reformed universe. It is a world that seems just barely possible. He is glad that she has come to make him see it.

living statues

You see him inside the subway station and feel the way you did when you gave him a dollar and he came alive. Startled, shy and elated. He's wearing a white t-shirt and jeans cut off at the knee, white grease paint on his face and white nylons under his cut-offs. His feathered wings are slung over his shoulder. Everything else—the halo, the robes, the offering jar—must be in his backpack. His hair is the color of orange rinds and his bare arms are almost as pale as his legs. You are two steps below him on the stairs leading up. You are one step below him, on the other side of the handrail, his wings arching over your head. He pulls ahead on the last flight. In the press of tourists and sidewalk evangelists, his wings flutter—he's moved them higher and closer to his body—and maybe it's because of this folding in that you somehow lose sight of him, finding yourself alone in the crowded square.

You are there to meet some college friends, to grab dinner at one of those awful places where you choose ingredients from an ingredient bar and then watch while the cooks sauté your food on a big open griddle. You are not comfortable enough with these friends to object to this restaurant, which is their unanimous choice. As you'd anticipated, they have better ingredient intuitions than yours: they take full advantage of all-you-can-eat while you leave plate after plate of sour-tasting stir fry in the center of the table. The bill arrives, the careful six-way splitting of costs, and then, on the way to the movies, you tell the story, again, of the time that you saw a late-night talk show host at this movie theater. It was Thanksgiving weekend, some years ago. He'd been with a man and a woman who looked just like him, and who went in the side door while he stood across the street, wearing a trench coat, waiting to be sneaked in. You tell your friends how the celebrity saw your mouth move when you whispered his name to X. He had turned then, and pulled his hat down over his face. He is very tall in real life, you tell your friends. Taller, even, than X. When you speak this name, your friends look away.

Have you heard from him? asks one—the boldest.

Not lately, you say. It has been months since you last dialed information, months since you last failed to find him. His things still turn up in odd corners of your apartment. He has gone abroad, he has gone to school—he has gone, that's the upshot of it.

The group decides on a comedy. You sit through scenes you feel you've seen before. Afterward, over ice cream, your friends paraphrase reviews that you've read, too. You used to write stories in college; they ask your opinion and then don't like it. They are medical students now, or bankers, or management consultants. You are a secretary. In matters of taste, they seem to have achieved consensus: they are pleased with anything supposedly clever. Why is it that you are not?

The conversation turns eventually to the small college from which you all graduated. There are many people here in the city who went to your school; there are parties regularly in parts of town that you don't know.

Why don't you ever come out, they say. What are you up to all the time?

One friend nudges your shoe with hers. I can't believe you still have those! she says. Remember sophomore year when everybody had those?

I don't know, you say. Call me next time.

I will, says the bold one, and touches you, briefly. We'll go shopping, too.

She's the one you're most anxious to get away from.

Together, like tourists, the group of you wanders through the square. Street performers are everywhere, strings of lights, balloons. Pick a card, a magician says, and extends his empty hand toward you as though fanning a deck. You whisper in a stranger's ear—you've picked the seven of diamonds. The magician shuffles your invisible card back into his deck, then pulls your card, incarnate, from his breast pocket. You have no idea how he knew—everyone who witnesses puts some kind of bill into his top hat. Throughout the plaza, crowds obscure the better acts; you stand on your toes to see them. When you finally spot a tall white pillar, you draw your friends near. Have you ever seen those people, you ask, the ones who stand very still and then come to life? They think you're talking about mimes at first, but then one of your friends who's traveled in Europe says that what you are talking about are living statues, and that these are common in Europe's major cities, these are nothing special. He tells you about the silver and gold people he saw in Florence, and now you are hoping that no one will turn around, to see your angel in his attitude of perfect anguish, waiting for someone to bring him to life.

Your friends decide against beers because someone not present is running a marathon the next morning and they are all going to watch. Come along, they say, but you shake your head no: you have to work. Call in sick, they say, and again, you say no—though already, you've decided that this is what you'll do. Not to join them along the marathon route, but to have an extra day for yourself. In the afternoon, you will come into the city, keeping below ground, as you sometimes do. You will ride the train until it floods with thin bodies cloaked in tinfoil capes. Everyone with a seat will stand so they can sit. You will watch the wrecked runners as they tear into parcels of food. The smell of bananas will fill the car, and then the fusty non-smell of energy bars. The foil capes will keep the runners warm, but in the interval while they are warming, their collective shivering will make a sound like wind chimes.

You walk toward the subway with your friends. At the top of the stairs, you stop and say, What night is this? Sunday? You deplore Sunday night television, telling them that you're just going to pop in to a bookstore—you'll see all of them next time, hopefully soon. A book sounds good, says one of your friends, let me come with you. But then he realizes what time it is, and that he only has five minutes until his bus, which comes but once an hour on Sundays. You smile until all of your friends are out of sight, then turn and rush back to the bricked plaza where the statue stood.

He's still there, moved only a few feet, a little bit closer to the crowd but still outside of the streetlights. He's standing with his hands folded in front of him, and his face is perfectly blank—disinterested, as an angel's should be. You take a bill from your purse and move toward him, very slowly. This is the difficult part, during which you feel like the performer. You are moving and he is still; you are the object of interest.

You stop just in front of him; he does not look down. His irises are like openings in the white of his face. You marvel at his unblinking eyes and wait, while slowly, his tears begin to well. A moment later, a miracle—they spill over, like a statue's weeping blood. You put your dollar in the offering jar.

He bends toward you, stiff like a marionette and with his eyes now fixed to yours. He parts his white hands and lifts them, gesturing to include the whole square, all of the people. He turns his palms toward the ground and draws them slowly in a circle around him, as though running his hands across the heads of children. When his hands are in front of him, outstretched and inches from you, he turns his palms up, bends his arms, and draws his open hands in toward his body. You step forward—you are close enough to remark the creases in his white lipstick, the moist pinkness of the corner of his eye. But he has frozen again, his eyes fixed beyond yours, his breath barely lifting the breast of his long robe.

You have been given what you paid for. He has even cried; it is more than you'd expected. Still, you wait. You try to stand as quietly as he is standing, the two of you become a tableau. Then you note the tearstains running down his cheeks—imperfections that you have caused.

You lay another dollar in his jar, and you hurry away as he begins to move.

You do not go far. From the top floor of a nearby bookstore, you can see the plaza clearly. You watch as, with his back to the building, he animates for each tourist who adds to his jar. They tend to approach him slowly, as though they too are unfamiliar with Europe and its living statues. You notice that he does not pull any of the other spectators toward him, and you understand that it was special, for you, that last gesture. You think of his eyes engaging yours, his expression in which there is nothing and everything.

When the bookstore closes at eleven, the crowd in the square has thinned. People have gone home, or into bars and restaurants, and from the bookstore's basement exit, you watch as the angel packs up his things. He collapses the stool on which he's been standing and places it in his backpack along with his robe and his halo and the offering jar. Stripped down to his t-shirt, he looks anemic, eccentric, with the wings over his shoulder and his glowing white face. You are at a magazine kiosk while he is at the bank—you can see him making a deposit in the vestibule, at the ATM. You shadow him down a side street, and when he sits on a slat-wood fence, you realize that you have reached his bus stop. The buses will stop running altogether in a half hour; his is not a bus route that you know.

You crouch behind a berried shrub. On the other side of town, your new roommate will be listening to music or talking on the phone, painting her toenails in a corner of the couch. She'll be baking bread or taking a bath, reading a novel or eating a snack. She'll be sure to ask, as soon as you've hung up your jacket, whether you had a nice time and how your friends are. Her day will have been good; her day, when detailed, will have been comprised of irreproachable recreations. Looking at him now, you feel relieved of all of that. He is still and separate, sitting just yards away on the rail fence. The sight of him braces you against the rest of your life.

When his bus pulls up, you board in a rush, as though you haven't been waiting there with him. He takes a seat by the window, just past the section reserved for the elderly. You sit on the other side of the aisle, in the last seat by the back door. The bus leaves the square and crosses the river. You pass row houses and stockyards, paying more attention to him. His wings are upside-down, with their arches resting on the tops of his feet and the wingtips just poking his chest. His hands lie still in his lap until, the white paint turned yellow by the bus light, his left hand rises to press the indicator strip. He walks to the front of the moving bus, is off as soon as it stops, so that you must vault from your seat and yell "back door" in order to keep up. The bus driver refuses to release the back door, since the bus is uncrowded, and by the time you've accepted this and made your way off the front, the angel is half a block ahead.

He leads you to a red brick apartment building with a name painted above its glass doors: The Crystal. You are outside, on the bottom step of his stoop, feigning a smoke while he checks his mail. The mailboxes are in the foyer; you can see which one he's opened. He passes through a second glass door into the lobby. You watch him mount the stairs, his slow ascent with the wings held toward you, hiding his face.

You wait on the stoop until someone else walks up to the building. You smile at this person, a stumble-drunk. He obliges you by holding the door. On your way in, you glance at the mailboxes. It was number 14—just one name on the box, though you can't stop to read it—the door is still being held.

You climb the stairs you watched him climb. The numbers lead you to the back of the building. Approaching his door, your legs begin to tingle, as if they are falling asleep still in motion. The corridor is quiet and empty, no neighbors to see how clumsy you've become, how haggard after this long evening. You will not be able to conceal these things from him.

Not a sound comes from his apartment—no voices, no music. Standing with your ear to his door, you hear nothing at all. You think: if you knock, he will surely speak. There is no other arena in which this might happen. It could never happen in the plaza, among strangers. It could never happen in costume. You imagine him close by—eye to peephole, even—willing you to take courage. You draw back your fist, and you knock.

You hear stirrings inside, slap of feet against floor. The door opens just wide enough for his head to wedge into the open space. His skin is pink and his hair is damp. He has dark eyebrows, many freckles. But his features are set in their familiar, resigned expression—and you are comforted to find that it is his natural one.

Hello, he says.

Hello, you say.

He watches you, waiting. You speak.

I'm your neighbor, you say. It comes to you quickly. I was wondering if I could borrow an egg.

After a moment, he nods. All right.

He closes the door. You think that he's left you in the hallway, but instead there is a scraping noise as he disengages the police lock. He opens the door all the way. You step inside the apartment. It's a studio—spare, as you would have guessed. Above the open futon hang his wings, a shade whiter than the wall. The kitchen is a narrow line of appliances. He crouches before the economy-sized refrigerator; its metal shelves reverberate as he shifts items around. His face is gaunt by refrigerator-light. He returns to you with a cool brown egg. His fingertips are warm when he places the egg in your palm.

I'm sorry to bother you so late, you say. I thought I had everything.

It's fine, he says. I just got in.

Thank you, you say. I'm making a cake. I'm making it now because I just got in, too. I thought I had enough eggs and then when I didn't, it was too late to go for more.

The supermarket's open 24 hours, he says. But maybe you don't like to walk at this hour.

No, you say. Not by myself.

I'm sorry to hear that. It's too bad when women feel afraid at night.

It's only sometimes, you say. You're kind to be concerned.

You glance around his bare room. I like your apartment, you say.

He raises his eyebrows. There are no chairs, no books, no pictures in the room behind him.

I like its simplicity, you say. I'm not materialistic, either.

Well, he says. My stuff's getting here next week.

You find that you do not recognize his face when his mouth is moving.

Did you just move in? you ask. I thought I'd seen you before.

He shrugs. I was traveling last fall, my things have been in storage—you know.

Oh, you say. Were you in Florence?

He smiles a little. I was a lot of places, he says. What kind of cake are you making?

You shake your head; you're finding it hard to breathe in this small room. Something from a box, you say. Duncan Hines.

But what flavor?

You panic. Devil's Food.

My favorite, he says, and he smiles wider. He looks younger than you and older, too. Did you need anything else?

No, you lie. You thank him. You thank him and move backward toward the door, only a few steps, and he's walking forward, so that you face each other like dance partners, paired, except that your hands are cupped in front of your sternum, cradling the egg.

Good night, he says. It was nice meeting you. You are in the hallway and he is in the apartment. I'll watch to make sure you get in okay.

There are four other red doors off this hallway; he believes that one of them is yours.

Oh no, you tell him, I live downstairs. No one was home on my floor, but I heard you walking. I can hear your footsteps, sometimes, through the ceiling.

I try to remember to take off my shoes.

Yes, you tell him. You're always very quiet.

Well . . . good luck with the cake. Maybe you'll bring me a slice when it's done.

Yes, you say, but you feel cheap for having lied. You paid him to come to life for you, and now you're lying while he listens. You edge toward him.

I don't really need this, you tell him. You hold it out to him. I'm not making a cake.

That's all right, he says, but his bowed body stiffens. Responsively, you lean forward.

I don't actually live here, you tell him.

Oh, he says. He frowns.

I took your bus, you say. I walked with you and when you got on, I did, too.

Is this a joke? He leans from the doorway, turns his head up and down the hall. Are you one of Jen's friends or something?

I wanted to see you tonight, you say. I thought it might help if I saw you.

I'm sorry, he says. I don't know you.

You do, you say. From earlier. I was the one who was alone—don't you remember? You cried.

His face is reddening. I'm sorry, he says. I think you're confused. I'm not . . . what you think I am.

You try to smile. I don't think you're an angel.

His expression doesn't change. Is there someone I could call to come get you?

No, you say. There isn't anyone.

He rubs his eyes. There is only the doorjamb between you. You reach for his hand, but he steps back.

A cab, he says. I can give you some money. Let me get my shoes and I'll walk you to the intersection.

Please, you say.

He does not look at you. You can't be here, he says. I'm sorry.

But you beckoned me, you say. It is a terrible word to have to say out loud.

He is shaking his head.

You did. Like this. You cannot look at him as you mime his movements, your hands outstretched, pulling him near. He is very pale now. Your eyes burn from not blinking. You drew me closer, you say. So I came.

You shouldn't have, he whispers.

Please, you say. Please.

He takes a deep breath. The air goes taut between you. He steps forward. His chest meets your fingers, curling them closed around the egg. His arms rotate in an arc abbreviated by the entryway. His hands fall cold on your shoulders. His eyes are bright and impassive, and yours shut as he bends toward you. In a moment, suspended, you feel insensate. Then his lips touch your forehead. Something turns over inside you like a boulder, dislodged and beginning to roll. You rise on your toes, reaching. But the air moves around you, the lock drops into place. When you open your eyes, you are alone again. The egg lies intact in your hand.

After a while, a radio begins on the other side of his door, wordless and lulling. It is late now—well after midnight. The buses have stopped. You've given away your last dollars. He'd offered you a cab—before he'd quite understood. You don't want it, now. The radio coughs, looking for a station; he knows that you are still there. You imagine him crouched in a corner, waiting. It's true that he is not what you thought he was—someone alone and open. But you can't blame him for that.

You secure the egg in your empty purse, and begin the long walk home.

mr. codman's women

It has been three days since Mr. Codman took off his pants. He wears his drawers to dinner, laying his handkerchief over his lap during meals. His wife and daughter seat themselves at the far end of the table. They don't care to sit too close to his elbows; he finds himself, these days, struggling with his knife and fork. He eats less, drinks more, and comes out all right in the balance.

Mr. Codman overhears remarks made in muttering, feminine tones. His daughter disdains him—once, in London, she refused to take his arm walking in to dinner. She refused him, his Josie. He can remember her as an imp in sausage curls, dragging her kittens around the house and stealing sugar. She used to sit with him while he cut and smoked his cigars; she used to hold a cigarillo, unlit, between her baby lips and prop her heels next to his. There'd been her brother, too, for a while, the youngest member of their gang, and then there'd been the bad time in Paris, with only Josie understanding the French doctors, and John Jr. getting thinner and thinner. When Johnnie died, Codman's wife had the audacity to cry. As though it hadn't been entirely her doing—their being in France in the first place, eating strange foods and walking in damp neighborhoods. And Codman had said to her then—what was it? Well, he'd told her the plain truth: if she hadn't had the kids, they'd have had better times all along. She might have lived with him as his mistress. That had been exactly what he'd said.

Mrs. Johnson is to him now what Mrs. Codman might have been. In Mrs. Johnson he has found beauty and charm, girlishness, decency. Mrs. Johnson spoils him as Mrs. Codman never has. He thinks of her bosom, her voice, her perfume; he shuts his eyes. Mrs. Johnson decanting the wine, Mrs. Johnson turning down the bed. She is delicious.

The feminine muttering increases in volume. He raises his head to see the Codman women stalking out of the dining room. His wife is a reproachful woman, whom his daughter has come to resemble. His daughter, who once rode horsey on his knee, now leaving him alone with his full plate. It should not be so. A man should not be made a pariah in his own home. His forefathers built this house, earned this fortune. *His* forefathers, whose portraits line this dining room, a gallery of bold Codmans. It is only thanks to him that his wife and daughter are Codmans at all. But before he can point this out, the women are gone.

Alone, Mr. Codman bends to his plate—and stifles a shriek! There is a face looking back at him from his potatoes—a nose and mouth in relief—terrible! He shoves himself quickly back from the table. His handkerchief flutters after him as he flees the room.

Darling baby, writes Mrs. Johnson, *dearest of men! It's too hard to go a whole week without seeing you! Can't you get away sooner? Won't you try for your Helene? I should love nothing better than a carriage ride with you in the park this Sunday! Only, I haven't anything to wear. Shouldn't you love to see me in a new dress? I know you should; I have been to the dressmaker already and forwarded the bill to your accountant. You won't think it too bold of me, I know—not of Helene who is your wife in spirit. Oh, how I wish I could live with you in that great house and keep you company in the evenings! We would do things in proper style, you and I, John darling. I send you every bit of my love, dearest John. I kiss you and kiss you! XOXO, Helene.*

The letter awaited him in his study. Written on pale peach paper, it is scented with the cologne he gave to Mrs. Johnson last week. He rereads it, then tucks the pages into the pocket of his great coat (which he habitually wears over his drawers). A second letter arrived in the same mail. Despite her attempts to disguise her handwriting, despite her omission of a return address, he knows it is from Mrs. Smyth-Hurst. There's no sloppiness about Mrs. Smyth-Hurst; he appreciates that about her, even if she is no longer his favorite. He breaks the seal on her letter.

John, she writes. *A disturbing story has reached me concerning you and that scandalous woman, the supposed "Mrs. Johnson." It is widely known that she is the widow of no one. I have most often heard her roots traced to Toronto, where it is said she managed a saloon. That is the nicest of the stories, be assured. I won't lower myself to repeat the others.*

You will appreciate that the Codman name is sullied by any such association. My own reputation, I hardly need say, is also jeopardized.

John, as you love me and your good name, I beg you to cut this woman.

Thank you for the sable you sent over Friday last; it is just the thing and what everyone is showing for next season. You are, as ever, a dear man.

I hope this finds you well.

Your affectionate, Cassandra Smyth-Hurst.

P.S. I have implemented your advice as to security windows on the garden floor and am most satisfied with the results.

Mrs. Smyth-Hurst is a woman of taste and it is gratifying to him how often their tastes coincide. He will never forget their first meeting, years ago at the gunsmith's shop. She had been still in her widow's weeds then, like a small, sad-faced child, turning in her gloved hands the most delicate of pearl-handled pieces. She felt vulnerable, she said, in her large house. The late Mr. Smyth-Hurst had hired the staff; she'd never quite trusted them. And then there was the matter of the neighborhood! A teacher's training college stood just down the block; she had a mortal fear of independent women. Mr. Codman had understood.

He writes quickly to both of his mistresses, making a date on Sunday to see Mrs. Johnson, a date on Monday to see Mrs. Smyth-Hurst. He is not inclined to answer Mrs. Smyth-Hurst's accusations in writing. She can scold and he, supplicate, once they are alone. Then, too, she is apt to brandish cunning little weapons. Mr. Codman takes a pull from his nipper. Clamps and gags and stoppers: he shivers to think of them.

Things are more straightforward with Mrs. Johnson. A pretty dress and she's satisfied. So is he. With her bright complexion and smooth limbs she is like one of the dolls that Josie used to unwrap on Christmases. He used to wonder at the child's delight in dressing and undressing her babies. Now he understands. But whereas little Josie tired of her Christmas dolls by Valentine's Day, he has been enraptured by Mrs. Johnson for six months now. He leans back and thinks of her dimpled cheeks and of the ticklish way she wiggles when he helps her into the carriage. On Sunday, they will roll together through the dowdy old park, laughing at the statuary, the ducks, the silly, conventional families out for their weekly strolls. Let those strollers stare! No doubt Mrs. Johnson will be the prettiest woman at the park, with her new dress and wafting hair. She is not shy about public displays. And with her beside him, neither is he. What is there to be ashamed of in the company of such a doting darling? Let eyebrows raise: he is a Codman, not some trembling businessman; his ancestors erected this park for their own pleasure.

Mr. Codman rummages through his pockets for his nipper. Mrs. Johnson will be decked out in blue silk, and he will look sporting beside her in his straw hat and . . . and what? His drawers? His greatcoat? He shoves back his desk chair, rushes to his dressing room, tears open his wardrobe. There must be something decent here but—how have his things grown so tattered? Shirts out at the elbows, suits greasy and dated. His best day suit was stained by Mrs. Johnson's poodle on their last outing. He spoiled the jacket of his second-best, laying it across a puddle for Mrs. Smyth-Hurst's convenience. How could he have forgotten? Dapper John Codman, with nothing to wear. He reaches deep in the wardrobe for his mourning suit. Perhaps with a pink boutonnière . . . he holds it up, steps in front of the mirror—screams! The suit is fine—too morbid for a drive in the park—but what is this substance on his face? A white crust, caked to his chops and his chin. A gritty paste, a concrete of sorts—perhaps someone tampered with his shaving lather? And now a delayed reaction, a poison weeping from his pores—he will suffocate! He dashes down the hall to the bathroom, bursting in on his wife. Out! she shrills. Out! As though he wanted to see her in buff—as though he wanted anything to do with her! Emergency! he yells. Murder, you witch! But she pelts him with her sponge. He slams the door and races away, down the back stairs, into the kitchen. He forces his head under the spigot. The water takes the concrete away, dissolves it immediately. He dries his face on a dish towel, falling into a kitchen chair. Safe.

The astonished housecats creep out from beneath the stove, and he strokes their backs. Good kitty, says Mr. Codman. That's a mouser. These are his daughter's aging darlings, whose names he once knew. Blackie? Snowie? Each had been christened years ago, at a ceremony held over the bird bath. Little Josephine clutching the cats in old table linens while he touched their heads with water and intoned about the Holy Spirit. They'd persuaded Johnnie that Mother didn't need to know. What fun they'd had back then, what conspiracies! Mrs. Johnson has a giant poodle called Saucepan—Saucie for short. She is the most charming woman of his acquaintance, Mrs. Johnson.

There is a scratching at the other side of the cellar door. Mr. Codman's hand snaps to the handle of his pocket pistol. Who is it? he calls. Move along, at once! He sidles from the table to the wall, extinguishing the electric light. The scratching continues. Be gone! Mr. Codman roars. He throws his bedroom slipper at the door, throws its mate. Shoo! he cries. The noise stops. His slippers are now on the far side of the room. He creeps toward them. He can hear the beast chirruping quietly. It is either a rat or an intruder making rat noises. More likely, he thinks, the latter. He slips his feet back into the damp interiors of his woolen slippers. Have strength, he tells himself. He thinks of Mrs. Smyth-Hurst, who is nervous of strangers but shoots sparrows from her bedroom window. He thinks of the determined look she gets before she takes a shot. She is so sure of hand! But her charms cannot compare to those of Mrs. Johnson. Mr. Codman shoves open the cellar door and fires. The chirruping beast flips head over paws down the stairs. It is neither man nor rat, but—he cringes—cat.

Mittens! shrieks Josephine from behind him. She is unnervingly quiet on her feet. She shoves Mr. Codman as she sprints past. I'll shoot *you*, you beast! You ought to be locked up!

Yes, declares another voice. Mr. Codman turns to find his wife standing on the threshold of the dining room. Her damp hair, lit from behind, emits a frizzled aura. You *ought* to be locked up, she says. She turns on her heel and glides away, silent as a ghost.

Mr. Codman drops his pistol on the kitchen table. His hands have begun to shake. He crawls to the cupboard beside the sink, drags Cook's bucket forward. She keeps her jug beneath the washrags. He has no idea what it is—whiskey or rye or applejack—but a swig always sets him right. He is sitting sprawled-legged on the floor when his daughter passes by with the cat. Let Father help you, he says. We'll bind that right up. As usual, she ignores him.

Mr. Codman is not at his best the next afternoon. He had been awakened that morning at an unreasonable hour. Cook's scream was his alarm. She had discovered him curled against the stove, his great coat having fallen open during the night. Goodness, sir, she repeated, after the initial fright. You shouldn't scream at an armed man, he told her. It is a lesson they go over almost weekly. Mr. Codman has long suspected that Cook is a bit daft, but her puddings are delectable.

Mr. Codman dresses himself to the best of his ability, in a pair of charcoal trousers frayed at the seam and a jacket of lighter gray pinstripe. He seems to have lost weight since the pieces were cut—the trousers are loose at the waist, the jacket slumps on his shoulders. Well, he has not eaten heartily in some months, not since the loss of his boon companion. He and Jack Whitcomb had met at the club back in '85 and dined together nearly every day thereafter. His wife had still been skulking around in mourning back then, three full years after

Johnnie's death; his morbid wife hated to see him enjoy himself, as he did with old Jack. During the Whitcomb era, that riotous half-decade, she made Josie eat with her in the upstairs parlor. Meanwhile, downstairs, each dinner became a contest. To what excesses had they pushed one another, he and Jack Whitcomb! But old Jack had given way in the end—not to dyspepsia, or cirrhosis, as they'd always joked he might, but to a brain stroke. The last he'd seen of Jack, the old fellow was lying, slack-faced, in a nursing home. He'd failed quickly; he'd died. Jack Whitcomb, his boon companion.

Mr. Codman pats his face briskly with cucumber water. He can't be tear-stained and soppy when he sees Mrs. Johnson. Sentimentality—*his* sentimentality—upsets her. He must be strong for her, he reminds himself. A poor widow, depending upon him for cheer, and for sustenance besides. He can't imagine what kind of man Mr. Johnson must have been, to have left his wife with so little.

It is almost 1:30 when Mr. Codman sets out for the park. Walking, he sees that his suit is not as matched as he'd hoped: the jacket is a bluish-gray, the pants closer to black. But his appearance can only lend greater brilliancy to hers—star of creation, darling woman. He hires a pair of white geldings and waits just inside the park gate. It is not long until he spots her in the distance. He ties the horses and hurries toward her.

The new dress is not blue at all but rose, with a very becoming décolletage. Her white furs look splendid against its warm hue; her lovely blond curls bounce and wave around her face. Beside her, Saucie is clean and white, and gambols when he sees Mr. Codman. There, boy, says Mr. Codman, catching the dog's paws before they touch his jacket. There's a boy. Mrs. Johnson smiles sweetly as he offers his arm; her gentle weight seems to buoy him. He takes the dog's leash in his free hand.

Mr. Codman, she says. And how do you like my frock?
She has exquisite taste; he is happy to tell her so.

I only hope you aren't depriving yourself for my sake,
she says, looking him over with a playful frown.

My dear, he says. I would wear a potato sack if it meant
you would have another such gown.

He helps Mrs. Johnson into the hired phaeton—for a
moment, her shapely rump is on a level with his face—and
then they are seated side-by-side, with her arm tucked
through his and Saucie behind them on the groom's seat.
The horses clip along, and all is just as he'd imagined it.

Mr. Codman returns home shortly before eight. He and Mrs.
Johnson had driven into the country; they had stopped at a
farm house for cider and to relieve Saucie. The farmer took
them for a handsome married couple (Mrs. Johnson of
course still wears her late husband's ring). Later, at a wayside,
at dusk, they had caressed beneath the carriage top. He visits
Mrs. Johnson at home on Thursdays; it is never soon enough.

He has missed Sunday dinner, as he often does. Cook
left a light for him in the kitchen, and he unlocks the back
door. He likes to play a game of entering the house as quietly
as possible. It is important that he know just how quietly it
can be done, so that he can train himself to detect the softest
noise. The Codman home will not be burgled, not while he
has breath in his body and a pistol in his pocket (and, against
those occasions when he is pocket-less, he has stashed
pistols in every room in the house).

Mr. Codman finds his plate in the oven. He is about to
bite into his yeast roll when he hears a distinct female 'shhh.'
He creeps to the door.

David . . . no . . . later . . . father . . . madness.

It can only be his daughter, whispering at this hour.
But—David?

Please, Josie . . . tonight? The man's voice is deep.

Yes, Josephine says. Yes.

Mr. Codman begins to perspire. There is a man in the house, conspiring with his daughter! It cannot be proper. She is twenty-four, old enough to have a lover, but he does not approve of a girl carrying on in such a clandestine manner. He taps the handle of his pocket pistol. Surely he could run this fellow off. What hold could Josephine have on a man that couldn't be broken with a bullet? Assuming that they are lovers and not something else. He heard her say 'father.' What could she mean, mentioning him? He hears their footsteps; he crawls under the kitchen table. He can only hope they won't notice him beneath its cloth.

Their two sets of feet pass his hiding place. Josephine is wearing crepe-soled slippers; it's no wonder she gets around so quietly. The man wears tall black boots, like a highwayman or a pirate. Absurd affectation! That his own daughter would condone such foppery! The back door opens; they say goodnight. Mr. Codman hears a soft smack as if of lips. His daughter is as shameless as her mother is frigid. Josephine turns the door's three locks—at least she is still conscientious in this respect—and then he hears the oven open and close. A small tsk sound.

Here is my plate, his daughter says. How odd of Cook to leave it out in the open, when I told her I wouldn't be back from the theatrical society until seven-thirty. Shall I sit down to eat? She lays hold of one of the chairs, shakes it. Its legs bump against Mr. Codman's ribs. No, says his daughter. It's nicer upstairs, I think. Goodnight, Blackie, she coos. Goodnight, Snowball. Goodnight—well, I don't guess there's any others around.

His plate lifts from the table above him. The light is extinguished and the door swings open and shut. Theatrical society, indeed! Apparently Josephine is his match for play-acting. Well, he is glad she has wit enough to be sly, if she cannot be sweet. But what a nice girl she was, once—in that long-ago time when Sunday was *their* day at the park. He dries his eyes on the tablecloth. When he is composed again, when he's sure that she's gone, he creeps from his hiding place. She has taken his dinner—a good joke on him. Perhaps he will find a way to tease her about it in the morning. He'll keep her secret, so long as they can reach an understanding about the apportioning of food. Mr. Codman rummages around the kitchen until he finds a wedge of cheese, some molasses cookies. If he must eat scraps he will eat them in style. He pushes through the swinging door, into the dark dining room.

Hello, Father, Josephine says.

He just manages to keep hold of his plate.

Hello there! In the scant light from the foyer, he makes her out, sitting tall and straight at the end of the table. Goodnight to you, he says.

No. Something gleams in her hands. Sit down, Father, and have your dinner with me. She laughs. Not much of a dinner, considering.

I haven't much of an appetite, my dear. He takes his place at the head of the table.

Did you eat with that huzzy?

His hackles rise at the word. I ate a light supper earlier, he says, with a good friend.

A very good friend, says his daughter. She waves her hand. She is holding one of his pistols. What can you be thinking, Father?

Those are for protection, he says. Not stage props.

I was asking about your friendships. I know what *this* is for.

She seems to be pointing the gun directly at him. Mr. Codman lays his own piece on the table. He raises his empty hands.

What's this about, Jo?

I hate to bother you with my expenses, Father, when I know your income is stretched so thin. But I'm afraid this time it's necessary. I need to take a long trip. For my health. And I need you to finance it.

At the word 'health,' Mr. Codman's stomach seizes. My dear—what do the doctors say?

His daughter laughs. The doctors have not been consulted.

Then what's the problem, Jo? You haven't been . . . indiscreet? He thinks of the man in the black boots.

No, Father. Her voice hardens. I leave because of your actions, not mine. I am *sickened* by the name Codman.

Well! He looks to the wall for succor, to the ranked portraits, hidden in the dark. You have nothing to be ashamed of in your name, Miss Josephine. Your grandfather was a senator.

And my father is a fool and a philanderer.

A fine allegation to make in the dark. But he breathes, calms himself. You're making mountains out of molehills, child. You'll stay right here and learn to let your parents mind their own business.

I'm asking for what I can as easily take, Father—as my inheritance.

Again, he sees the pistol waver up from the table. She is likely hysterical. He thinks of offering Cook's jug, but thinks better of it.

Josephine, he says, quietly. Where do you reckon you'll go? Don't tell me that you want to be a governess or some foolish thing.

I will go with David, she says. He'll act, and I'll manage him, and we'll get by on the money from you and what he earns.

An elopement? I won't hear of it.

It's not for you to decide, she says sharply. But I won't marry David. Nor any other man I've known. However, as *you* must know, the appearance of it helps one get by.

And if I won't give you the money?

I heard a noise, says his daughter. I came downstairs. I saw you struggling with a burglar, and your gun went off. But it didn't hit the burglar.

I see, says Mr. Codman. Do you think you could hit me?

Beside his head, a mirror shatters. The report echoes back from the stairwell.

His ears ring. I see. Then your mother must be in on this, too?

Mother's out like a light. She takes to her laudanum like you take to your whiskey.

Mr. Codman rubs his ears. Since when?

Oh, Father! Josie scoffs. How else is she to sleep through your shenanigans? 'Hark' every ten minutes and 'fire' and 'alarm!' It's enough to wake the dead.

The expression hangs between them like gun smoke. He can't see Josie's face, can't see whether there is any sadness there, or mercy.

I would miss you, he ventures. My own girl.

You might have thought of that sooner. Her voice is still clipped and angry. Will you give me the money, and live—or not?

Mr. Codman sighs. It's yours.

Something heavy slides toward him. His checkbook.

Cook keeps a pen in the kitchen, Josephine says.

He lets his daughter bully him into the next room and signs away $1000. It's the better part of his liquid assets. The house consumes his monthly dividends and Mrs. Codman swats him away from her own fortune. He will make do; there is always a way to wheedle funds from his trusts—the money will grow back, as it were. But under the kitchen light his daughter is dressed for travel. She checks her watch—Johnnie's gold pocket watch—and he understands that she will leave immediately. His child.

Will you write to your mother? he asks. Will you let her know where you have gone?

She shakes her head. If in a few years I come through with a traveling show, I'll send word then.

She will feel this terribly, says Mr. Codman. Pray for her, sometimes.

His daughter snorts. I'll pray for her to learn temperance and leave you.

Well, he says. When did Josephine become so cool and hard? Maybe you'll pray for your father.

What can God do for you? Didn't he already tell you not to covet your neighbor's wife? And you've decided it's all right, anyway.

Mrs. Johnson is a widow, he says. And so is Mrs. Smyth-Hurst.

She blinks at him. Father, she says, you astonish me.

Goodbye, dear. He opens his arms to her.

Goodbye, she answers, picking up her carpet bags. I hope you'll be happy, at least—as I shall.

She unbolts the three locks, and is gone.

Mr. Codman wakes the next morning with an immediate sense of dread. What has changed? He reviews his losses: Johnnie, dead of pleurisy; Jack Whitcomb, lost and gone. And now Josephine, run off. The list only increases. Who is there left that loves him? Who is there left to love?

He splashes his face at the basin, dons his slippers and his great coat. He's slept late, but Cook will have saved the bottom of the coffee pot for him; Cook might be persuaded to make him some toast. He takes a great pull from his bottle of cheer. There's only Cook left to care for him.

She stops shelling peas when he enters the kitchen. Sir, she says, rising from the table. You'll want some breakfast. An egg, perhaps?

He frowns. Cook doesn't approve of late breakfasts. Toast, he says. Just my toast will do.

Of course. She hurries to the counter, cuts two thick slices from the loaf. It is not like her to be so brisk and solicitous.

Cook, says Mr. Codman. Is something the matter?

She puts the bread under the broiler and turns to face him. Sir, she says. I don't like to be the bearer of bad news, but I don't know where the missus has gone, nor when she'll be back.

Is something wrong with Mrs. Codman? Why wasn't I wakened?

No, sir, says Cook. It's not Mrs. Codman. It's that no one knows what's become of Miss Josephine.

What's become of Josie? What d'you mean?

Cook grips the rim of the sink. When the maid went to her room this morning, there was a ladder of torn sheets hanging out the window, and a postcard from Niagara mostly burned up on the hearth. Mrs. Codman's gone to the police station, sir.

Rather obvious. But who besides him knows the true extent of Josephine's cunning? Who besides him would question her apparent carelessness? He takes a seat, as if overcome.

My daughter, he groans. It is too much, Cook. But are you sure she's run off? Perhaps she just left the house early this morning?

Perhaps, sir, but it looks very much like an elopement. I'm terrible sorry, sir.

If this is the scene Josie has concocted, he will take up his role. He waves away the toast that Cook sets before him.

Who is the young man? he asks. If she's eloped, there must be a young man missing, too.

Of course, sir, and the missus thought of that. She's after the police to investigate the matter, but they say there's not much they can do yet with Miss Josephine only gone one night. I'm dreadfully sorry, sir.

And a note? Did she leave any word?

Cook shakes her head. Only that burned-up postcard. It's a sad case, Mr. Codman.

He nods. What would he be feeling right now if he hadn't seen her last night, in her traveling suit, in her theatrical mood?

Cook, he says, what happened to the dining room mirror?

Oh, sir! I'd nearly forgotten. That's the principal reason that Mrs. Codman has gone to the police station. When I came in this morning, I found the mirror shattered. By a bullet, sir. And one of your pistols lying here on the kitchen table.

Then she's been kidnapped, he says, and senses Josie nodding from the wings.

Cook wipes her eyes. It's a terrible thing, sir. And with all the precautions that you take—why, didn't you hear anything last night?

Mr. Codman shakes his head. The house was quiet when I came home. I left off my rounds at eleven because I'd grown so unaccountably tired. If only I'd stuck to my routine!

Mr. Codman! Cook cries. You were drugged! Of course you were, to have slept through a gunshot and Lord knows what else! Sir, we must call the doctor right away!

Mr. Codman furrows his brow and nods. Quite so, he says. It will be quicker, though, and perhaps better for me, if I go there myself, straightaway. He takes a desperate bite of toast. Thank you, Cook, for your counsel.

He hurries upstairs. What has he done? He's played his part—he's played dumb—and now how will he explain that check? Well, Josie could have forged his signature. Or, if he *was* drugged, perhaps he made it out in a stupor. But the bank will never pay it, if Josephine's disappearance is ruled a kidnapping . . . unless of course he acts the magnanimous father—'the money may help my dear daughter; *that* is the important thing.' As for the drugging . . . didn't Jo say that her mother kept laudanum? He pauses outside his wife's room, listens closely. He can hear the maid humming in his study. He slips quickly through his wife's door. The bottle sits on her dressing table, nearly full. He takes a great pull from his bottle of cheer, and replaces what he's drunk with a strong dose of the opiate. In the evening he will notice a strange taste, and submit the bottle to the investigators as evidence. He adds a few drachms of water to his wife's medicine. Is he helping his daughter or not? *Should* he help her?

It is noon by the mantel clock, and he is not yet dressed for his engagement with Mrs. Smyth-Hurst. How much can he tell her? She is so discreet, and yet . . . And yet it might be best to keep the truth of it to himself. Assuming, of course, that what he knows *is* the truth. There is nothing for him but to wear the mis-matched grays again. He combs his chops, pats his throat with scent, and rushes down the stairs.

She must be sent away, Mrs. Smyth-Hurst is saying. There can be no real question on that score, John. You'll find her a nice private clinic and say she's gone off visiting.

Mr. Codman paces the hushed Smyth-Hurst sitting room. He can't eat her finger sandwiches today; he can't stomach her damned mineral water and her nervous hands. He has told Mrs. Smyth-Hurst simply that Josephine has run away.

Cassie, he says. I don't believe that they'll find her.

Of course they will, says Mrs. Smyth-Hurst. Where could a girl like her hide? She's gone to the city, thinking to lose herself, but the police have enough sense to check the obvious places first. She's in a cheap hotel, under a false name.

Well, says Mr. Codman. But what if she's disguised herself?

Oh, what if? says Mrs. Smyth-Hurst. What if she's cut her hair, or dyed it? What if she's wearing men's clothes, or speaking with a Scottish accent? She can't keep it up forever, John. These girls act bold, but they always get their comeuppance.

Mr. Codman bites his tongue. It is his own fault that Mrs. Smyth-Hurst should dare to speak of his daughter so—as though she were a common schoolgirl, and not a Codman.

May I have a brandy tonic? he asks, in a strangled way. She mixes him a weak one and he tosses it back. She may have run off with anyone, says Mr. Codman. A gypsy or a circus clown, or *an actor*. He gives Mrs. Smyth-Hurst a significant look.

Even so, says Mrs. Smyth-Hurst. Even so. Did you hear that the minister's daughter has been recovered? And she'd gone quite native, out west. They found her wearing a deerskin and answering to a heathen name.

And they brought her back?

Kicking and screaming, Mrs. Smyth-Hurst affirms. They're giving her bromides and teaching her English all over again.

He swirls the dregs of his brandy. In such a case, Mr. Codman says, wouldn't it be better to let the girl alone?

Oh, John! says Mrs. Smyth-Hurst. Can you bear the thought of your grandchildren growing up in the gutter? A girl is never choosing just for herself, however much she may wish to think so. Your daughter has behaved with gross indelicacy, and you must correct her! You are still her father, are you not? I will not pretend, says Mrs. Smyth-Hurst, that you are blameless in this disaster. You must see now that this Johnson association is beneath you. It lowers you in the esteem of any *sensible* person.

Mr. Codman harrumphs. He draws his nipper from his coat pocket, then remembers the laudanum and puts it away. He pictures what she's described: a Codman child busking in the streets—or Josie on a golden prairie, with the open sky above her. His head has become an empty drum.

Mrs. Smyth-Hurst lays her hands on his shoulders. She is as small as a girl, as small as Josephine was, at sixteen, on their Grand Tour. He danced with his daughter in five European capitals before Johnnie took sick . . . before Josie knocked aside his arm on that last night in London. Those had been Jo's first ball dresses and she'd been so embarrassed and proud. Mr. Codman puts his hands now on Mrs. Smyth-Hurst's waist, draws her to him gently. She is no bigger around than a girl, and Jo had a white dress for her coming out; Jo's hair wouldn't take a curl but it looked just right anyway, done up in loops and swirls, and her eyes nearly popping out of her head from excitement. He had been her best beau, then—and now she's gone, his daughter, his first-born, his only living child. He wraps his arms around Mrs. Smyth-Hurst, he squeezes her, he cannot stop himself from breaking down weeping in her skinny little arms.

Days pass with no developments. No one answering to Josephine's description has been spotted in Niagara. No news has come from investigators elsewhere, and Mr. Codman begins to believe that his daughter will get away with it. She will outrun them all—the decaying Codman he faces in the mirror, the distinguished Codmans hanging the walls. His own father takes pride of place above the dining room mantel. Augustus Codman—the picture of liberality! Perceiving that his son was no banker or statesman, Augustus had carried on with that work and left John Codman to find his own way. Now it is *his* turn to let Josephine live in the world. Such permissiveness is hard, in practice, but he bolsters himself by consulting his father's frowning face. *To each his own* had been Augustus's motto. Codman strains now to recall that graveled voice. Instead he is fixed by his father's heavy gaze. No matter what Augustus had said, he'd rested his hopes for the family business on John Junior. Why else sell the bank so suddenly after the boy died; why else truck off to California at age seventy? Thanks to his father, Mr. Codman can't even find distraction in a sham job at Codman Bank & Trust. Instead he spends his afternoons shut in the dining room, mulling Josie's secret. Meanwhile, his wife drives daily to the police station. She seems to expand under a new sense of self-importance. Her lady-friends dine at the house most nights, and Mr. Codman is forced to put on his britches or vacate his seat at the table.

His routine is disrupted in other ways, too. Mrs. Smyth-Hurst has gone to the country for a fortnight; it is where she learned to handle a gun, she's told him. Their parting had been strained. It is unclear whether he will continue with Mrs. Smyth-Hurst when she returns. The Johnson affair is one thing; the scandal of a runaway daughter is another, in her eyes. He tried at first to carry on as usual. I've been a very bad boy this week, he'd confessed at the start of their last meeting. But instead of leading him to the bedroom, she'd just nodded. At the end of an awkward quarter-hour, she'd shaken his hand without taking off her gloves, and invited him to call on her visiting day, once she'd returned to town. He tells himself that he does not mind this loss—she is showing the smallness of her character by cutting him now. Still, it would have been manlier to have instigated the break himself.

Mrs. Johnson is the same darling as always. She surprises him with new dresses on Sundays, and with the most charming lingerie on Thursday evenings. Her concoctions are bewitching—now black satin, now virginal white, now a series of straps and garters that he cannot make sense of unassisted. But something is different. Well—*he* is different. He cannot exercise moderation, these days, with the champagne she always has waiting. Whereas before he did his best to split the bottle evenly, now he swills most of it while she is undressing—and then apologizes, again and again, when he is of no use to her. My baby, she calls him, and nurtures him tenderly. Her restorative potions give him indigestion; her mouth does not move him. He tries his best to mount her, with his head swimming and his stomach clutching, but, ever since Jo ran off, he has been forced to admit defeat. Thursday nights, often as not, he's prostrated on Mrs. Johnson's chaise lounge, nipping off a bottle of bourbon and weeping for the good old days. Saucie licks his face and Mrs. Johnson rubs his temples with cologne. One evening as they are enacting this sad tableau, he notices another change.

What is this? He sits upright and snatches the bottle of scent from her hand.

I'm surprised at your forgetting, she laughs, when you picked it out for me, special!

I never did! The cologne he holds has a tawdry scarlet label and an underlying smell of rubbing alcohol.

Then it must have been the bottle I bought myself, she says. The druggist recommended it when I purchased your . . . goatweed.

He tosses it into her lap. I wish you'd get rid of it and use what I gave you.

Of course, darling, she says. It was silly of me not to. Your lovie only wants to make you comfortable.

But had she just been silly? Or is Mrs. Johnson sly, too? What might she hope to communicate to him, by soothing his head with that cheap cologne? He is not such a simpleton—or such a prude—that he imagines her not to have other friends, but it is unsettling to think that they might be of a common order. The kind of men who can only spare second-best presents to their mistresses. He will watch her for other such lapses; he will be on his guard against Mrs. Johnson, too. He lets himself indulge in another fit of weeping, there on the velvet chaise with his head in her lap. What is left for him now?

Fully three months pass this way, in doubt and secrecy and mourning lost friends. Mr. Codman adds Mrs. Smyth-Hurst to his list of dearly departed. She is, after all, as good as dead to him. And Mrs. Johnson . . . well, with Mrs. Johnson, he is now on a death-watch. Meanwhile the $1000 sits in his bank account, accumulating interest. When will Josephine cash it? Or is she so flourishing, having left him, that even his money is useless to her?

Mrs. Codman devotes herself to a society for wayward girls. It is closing the barn door when the horse is already loose, but it keeps her busy, and Mr. Codman does not reproach her for her interest. Her absence makes the house seem bigger. He resumes his daily patrol of the fine old rooms, checking the window latches, the state of his pistols. On one such circuit through the parlor, he finds the maid sniffling over family photos. Both gone! the poor girl sobs. She holds a tinted portrait of the two children, gray overshot with lurid pinks and yellows. What an object to weep over, and yet Mr. Codman does his best to offer comfort. It is hardly proper to console a woman while wearing one's drawers and great coat—and then it is not proper at all, whether done in the parlor or the green bedroom or the linen closet. Mr. Codman learns to look past the maid's rough knees, her freckles. She is most adept at *un*-making the beds, he is happy to find—and if he fails to perform, she shrugs her thin shoulders: that's one less set of linens to bleach.

Mr. Codman is thus surprised to find his wife at home one afternoon when he returns from the club and the tailor's. His quarterly dividends have come in; he is finally seeing about new suits; he has paid up his club dues and re-opened his tab. John Codman, he'd reminded the bartender, in a voice loud enough for the new members to hear. Let others come and go: he *will* be himself again.

Oh, John, Mrs. Codman says, as soon as he comes through the door. She is sitting, unaccountably, in the foyer. Here you are reeking of alcohol, and we have to get to the station just as quickly as we possibly can!

Looking up at him, his wife seems almost young: neck stretched taut, eyes liquid and bright. For a moment she could be a girl again. And maybe, too, her playfulness has returned. Mr. Codman smiles: Are we taking a trip?

Not the train station, you fool, the *police* station! They've found her, John—they've found Josephine at last—only, she won't own up to it, and they want us to come down and make an identification. Oh, John, I am trembling all over—feel my hand—and what will we do if she won't know us? John, say something!

Well, he says. His stomach feels peculiar. Where has she been?

They found her in Sault Saint Marie of all places; they say she's gone thin and wild; she'd been left behind by a traveling show, half-dead with pneumonia. Oh, John—if we had lost her, too!

His wife is clutching his arm with her thin, strong hands. It may have been years since she's touched him.

She's back, says Mr. Codman. Well, Susan, we must go to her.

Yes, says his wife. Oh, hurry!

The carriage has been waiting for him—Mr. Codman suspects that his wife is afraid to see their daughter alone. In truth, so is he. He had thought her sly enough to get away with it; he had hoped for it. Hoped that Josie might make a fresh start of things, away from her mother's influence. Well, it could happen still. After all, because she's back doesn't mean they will be able to keep her. He will not consent to locking her up, if that's what Mrs. Codman has in mind. And if she has in mind to send them both away . . . it will be his word against his wife's that he is of sound mind. A Codman's word means something, after all.

The carriage draws up in front of the station; one of the detectives is at the curb to greet them. Mrs. Codman, he says. The girl has been ill with fever—and I must caution you that you will find her altered.

We have expected as much, says Mrs. Codman. Please, we are ready.

The same talon-hand that held him before takes hold of Mr. Codman's forearm. They are ushered past the desk and into an interrogation room. And then the women's matron is brought in, with Josephine.

Only, it is not Josephine.

Mr. Codman feels his spirits lifting, so that he seems pressed against the ceiling of the dingy room. What a mistake! His wife does not see it at once, she takes this poor creature's hand, and repeats Jo's name, quietly. But the girl only blinks, the girl with pocked skin and a furtive way of glancing around. In the acting troupe, she must have played a crone, with her terrible posture and hollowed cheeks. This is not his quick daughter, no matter that she was found with Johnnie's gold watch. They are the same size, yes, their eyes are the same blue—but this urchin is no more his daughter than the warden is.

Is it she? asks the detective. She was signed in to the last two hotels as J. Codman.

Mr. Codman laughs aloud. His daughter, so careless as to use her own name!

They are somewhat like, says Mrs. Codman. She squeezes the girl's hand again. What is your name, dear?

It's Susan Montgomery Codman, answers the girl, baring her teeth in a smile.

His wife stumbles backward. This is her own full name, of course.

What's that, asks Mr. Codman. What's that again?

As if you didn't know, the girl says. She crosses her arms.

Does she have Josephine's mark? his wife asks the matron. A strawberry birthmark, on the back of her neck?

The matron turns the girl and lifts her black, bobbed hair to show a nasty scar.

Looks as if she's had it removed, ma'am.

No, says Mr. Codman. Anyone could have a wound like that—a boil, a bite.

Ma'am? asks the detective.

Mrs. Codman begins to weep. I don't know! Josephine, if it is you, won't you tell us plainly?

The girl only smiles. Her teeth do not look like Josephine's. Several on the bottom row are chipped. There is nothing familiar about her, head to toe. And yet . . . under what circumstances would Jo have parted with her brother's watch?

John, Mrs. Codman begs. John, do something!

Was anyone with her? asks Mr. Codman. He rubs his chops. Perhaps—a man?

John! gasps his wife.

Well, ma'am, there was somebody—we've got him in the holding cells. A fellow named David Tucker.

Yes, says Mr. Codman, that's right.

Pardon? asks his wife.

May I see him? asks Mr. Codman.

The detective leads Mr. Codman away from his gasping wife, down a narrow corridor, then unlocks him through to the holding cells. At the end of the line, by himself, waits a tall man with ridiculously long hair. He is not wearing boots.

Tucker! barks the detective, and the man stands. Mr. Codman to see you.

They face each other through the bars.

You were with that girl, says Mr. Codman.

Tucker nods. I was. His deep voice resonates from the stone walls.

What is her name?

Sir?

That girl's name—do you know it?

Sir, her name is Josie Codman.

No, says Mr. Codman. Her real name.

I suppose it's Josephine, sir, but I'm surprised at your asking.

Mr. Codman shakes his head. Mr. Tucker, he says. I'd like a straight answer. My daughter left with you; where has she gone?

Tucker frowns. I don't wonder at your not knowing her, sir, with her hair dyed and . . . and she's been sick for some time. I tried to send her home when she first started coughing, but she's stubborn, you know. I thought if I put her name on the register somebody might see . . . and now here I am like a kidnapper. We've both been awfully hungry, sir—so if you could see about sending some food back, I'd be in your debt.

But you're already in my debt, says Mr. Codman. If your story is true. What have you done with her money—the money I gave her?

Money? Tucker blinks. There never was any money, sir. We was in a hotel fire in Ladysmith, Wisconsin, and after that we had just the clothes on our backs. And I've been hungry for months now, sir, what with medicines and always sparing the best for her, so if you could just see about some food—

That'll do, says the detective. Mr. Codman's head throbs—what is it lately that's always wrong with his head? There's not much to Tucker—he seems thin enough to slide through the bars of his cell. But the story is growing plumper. Could his daughter—his dear one!—really have survived such mean conditions? Not a prairie or a garret but a scrabbling, itinerant existence. Mr. Codman is scarcely aware of the detective pulling him along and then he is in the examination room again. His wife has been given a chair, given salts; she is having trouble bearing up. And the girl is still standing, with her back to him. She's holding herself up more proudly now, head high, and he begins to make out Josephine in her—his unrelenting girl. They will take her with them—they can't leave her in jail with common criminals. The Codman house—*his* house—will have to accommodate her.

Josie, he says, and the girl turns to him. Her eye twitches.

He steps toward her. Father and Mother have been worried about you. We're glad you are back. And now . . . well, you must regain your strength. We'll take you to the mountains, get you some good mountain air. He coughs; he straightens his tie. We'll take care of you, Jo.

What more can he say to her? He can think of nothing—
he can't continue. He has begun to shake, but he doesn't
reach for his nipper. Whatever this is, he must bear it: he
is, after all, a Codman. And maybe she is, too. An actress, a
diplomat, a banker: everything that he has never been. Mr.
Codman moves closer to the girl. He looks down at the
chestnut roots of her tar-black hair; he traces the blackened
curve of her eyebrows. It has been many years since he has
been in the world with his daughter, many years since she
refused to know him. He adjusts his lapel, he checks the
buttons of his jacket. He offers her his arm. The girl reaches
out with her thin, familiar hand—and when he begins to
weep, she pats him, not unkindly.

the mission

Once there was a girl, who pressed her ear to the wall and listened to the tick, tick inside of it. Once there was a family story: grandparents, a farm house, a faulty toaster turning everything to ash. *You don't have to worry about that,* a mother said. *Old wires,* a father added. But every house has a box of wires tacked to its outside. If a man were to creep out of the woods and cut those wires, sparks might fly. Or if an animal were to go rabid, eyes rolling, mouth foaming, it might slice with its teeth through those candy-colored threads. The house would fall black and inside the walls, wires would smolder. Only the girl would hear their fine crackle. She circled the breaker box, afternoons, after school. She pressed her ear to the box's metal door. *Leave me alone,* she told her twin brother, again and again. And, in other moods: *plug this in for me.* How he yelped if a stripped cord zapped him. A puff of smoke between them.

What is it, what is it? her parents surely asked. They took her to other adults, who asked the same question, less plainly, asking her to draw pictures, play with dolls, take computer tests. *It* was the ticking the girl heard in the wall, the beating that came through her pillow at night—like an army of footsteps, nearing. *What is it*: the expression on her brother's face, when again she tricked him into trusting her. He never tattled, ever—and never would.

Once there was a girl, she told her brother, who lived where this house stands, a long, long time ago. A girl from the era of missions.

An Indian girl? He eyed her warily. Or a missionary?

Whichever you want.

But he would demand that *she* pick, and her story would take shape: A white girl.

A white girl, she told him, whose parents brought her here when there weren't roads or stores, just trails and trees and animals and Indians. And her parents were scared of all that; they built a house. At night they huddled under their blankets while the girl sat up listening to a tick, tick in the walls.

From bugs?

No—and not mice, either. Not the house settling or the wind outside. It was a sound coming from the girl's ear, like the sea from a shell.

Bugs in her ear? Her brother was her twin, but he was not quick.

What ticks?

A watch?

What else?

. . . a stopwatch?

A bomb, she told him. A bomb.

You said this was old-fashioned times, her brother said. They didn't have bombs.

Cannonballs are like bombs. Musket shells.

Those don't tick.

Well—this girl's head was a bomb, okay? And she didn't like having to be a missionary.

Didn't she believe in God?

She didn't like *having* to. She didn't like her parents pushing their beliefs on people. On the Indians. On her. She didn't like being pushed.

How old was she? her brother would want to know. Did she have a brother? Where did she go to school? Didn't she *have* to do what her parents said?

The girl shook her head. You were right: that sound in her ear *was* like a watch, and every tick she heard was another second spent just doing what she was told. Her parents didn't like it when she put her ear to the wall and they didn't like it when she had visions—that means ideas. They thought they knew better than her.

Didn't they? Her brother's face showed her what she would look like, if she ever looked confused.

What do you think?

He squirmed then, as he did on the rare Sundays when they went to church. If we played that, you could be the girl, and I could be one of the Indians.

Native Americans, she told him. She nodded: I'll play that. First we need to go to the trading post.

The girl led her brother to the kitchen, toward beef jerky and the brown bottles kept above the refrigerator. They didn't have refrigerators in olden times, she told him, positioning the stepstool. Kids drank whiskey back then.

No, he would certainly have said.

For toothache and croup and whatever. You have a cold, don't you? The white people gave you fire water.

And he would have reached up to take the bottle she handed down. What she poured, he would have drunk, a whole mugful. When she saw that he'd had enough, she would have continued.

You're the Native American boy, she told him, in her voice that made any story exciting. You've come to get me, so that we can run away.

But I like my parents. They let me have my own canoe.

Well . . . She closed her eyes. What if you pretended something different?

Her brother would have wobbled a little then, breathing through his mouth. He would have reached out his hot, sticky fingers and traced bands on her cheeks, as if with war paint. Okay, he would have said.

We won't be able to run away if my parents catch us, she told him. So let's play that I hid bones from the midden pile in my cot, and later they'll think that was me. And then here's what we do. She found a cleaning rag under the sink, pushed it down the neck of the whiskey bottle. This is our lantern, she told him. She took a lighter from the junk drawer. We have to go outside to play the rest. Her brother would still have been able to walk, sort of. Let's hide up on the hill, she told him, pushing him in that direction. Let's hide behind the big tree.

Together?

Yes. But first I'll take my flint—she clicked the lighter's button—and create a distraction.

The rag caught fire, flame flaring from the bottle's neck. The bottle arced through the open kitchen door. The girl pulled her brother away from the house—away from the blazing puddle on the linoleum and the promise, soon, of the smoke alarm. He might have laughed as she dragged him drunk through the trees. It might have been the fall of the year—it must have been. Leaves were deep everywhere in the woods, a dry pile that she pushed together with her feet and hands, panting. Her brother would have been sick, rolling on his side to vomit. After she cleaned him, she would have buried him under those leaves and crept in beside him. The leaves soft around them, the dark pulsing with their breaths. She pressed her ear to his neck and heard his heart beating—that steady, ceaseless tick. Beneath her thumb, the lighter clicked again.

the sweeper

There's no such thing as . . ."

"*What?*" But I'm awake, my dream dissolved. I lie still, straining after details. What was happening, what would I have understood if I had stayed asleep a second longer?

I push my sleep mask up my forehead. Still dark. I remember a man's calming voice, my own eagerness. Why do I always wake up too soon?

"—does not exist," the same voice says, firmly.

"What did you say?" I sit up, reaching for my lamp. But I can tell that the man is not in the apartment, or in my head. His voice came from the street. I crawl to the edge of my bed and peer through the blinds.

"There is no such thing as—" A vehicle is turning onto the street, a big, white, blunt-nosed truck. A street sweeper. Its headlights play off the tightly packed brownstones. Speakers are mounted to the top corners of its cab. "—does not exist," it announces again. The missing word is at the same frequency as the truck's spinning brushes.

I push my window open to hear better. Up and down the street, people are leaning out like me. A few hands extend cellphones over the sidewalk. By the time I find mine, the truck has reached the end of the block. Only then can I hear my neighbors, shouting across our Brooklyn street like it's 1935.

"What the fuck was that?"

"*What* did it say?"

"'There's no such thing as humans.'"

"'Demons'—'demons'!"

"It didn't say shit. Somebody's just messing with you."

"Fuck Brooklyn."

The recording comes again, less robust, playing back through somebody's phone. "There's no such thing as _____," it says. A blank where meaning should be.

"That's some PoMo bullshit right there," yells my downstairs neighbor. He's a first-year in the English PhD program at CUNY. I feel his window slam shut, directly below mine. Then there's a click, an eruption of tinny sound. Not the truck coming back, but my alarm going off.

On the subway, at work, everyone is talking about the sweepers. Everybody heard them—those of us in Brooklyn, Queens, the Bronx, Manhattan, Staten Island, Jersey City, Newark . . . even the middle managers who come in from Long Island and Connecticut. Like summer ice cream trucks, street sweepers seem to have canvased the greater metropolitan area, all playing the same spotty recording.

I work for a standardized test preparation company. We write fake standardized tests; we compose reading comprehension passages and fill-in-the-blank sentences for a living. But though we all seem to have heard the same thing, there is no agreement about what that voice said or meant. We cluster nervously in the centers of our pods, four-person cubicles, ostensible "creative spaces" in which we normally sit oriented to the corners. We've gone through endless coffee K-cups and even more theories by the time the PA system gives its long beep.

"Management is aware of the incident many of you experienced this morning," says a man's nasal voice—not *the* voice. "At this time, there will be no disruption of ordinary business. Our clients are relying on us to help them outsmart the test-makers. Are we going to let them down because of some prankster?"

"Go team!" urges the voice on the PA, and some of us answer in kind. But the announcement only prompts us to work on this problem individually. All day I look busy, as I list words that might fit the sweeper's blank space. Two syllables—I think. Maybe a terminal -n sound. *Heaven, semen, hoping, dreaming. Women, passion, children.* I am a writer, not just of standardized tests but of fiction (*fiction?*). I moved to New York ten months ago, after finishing my MFA; I moved to New York along with two-thirds of my classmates and who knows how many others, from how many other writing programs. Since then everything I've written has been like this list: not right.

"I heard 'U.N.,'" swears my podmate, Lara. The daughter of U.S. diplomats, she witnessed some bad stuff during her childhood deployments. Now she chairs the office's emergency preparedness squad. All day she wears her orange vest, her supply room keys on a lanyard around her neck. "Or maybe it was 'Yemen,'" she says. So far there's nothing in the news. "Figures," Lara says. "Stay ready."

We had to evacuate the office once before during my tenure, then because of a blackout. The lot of us milled about Bryant Park for twenty minutes with dozens of other displaced office workers. Then Lara passed out our water rations and we began walking home.

Today we wait for some other catastrophe.

But nothing happens. I clock out after doing even less work than usual, put in my time at the gym, and pick up dinner on the way home. I say hi to my roommate, the cousin of a high school friend, before she heads off to her boyfriend's for the night. Everything is as usual. And so it continues.

Every morning I wake up just before my alarm to the same calmly delivered, unintelligible message. "____ does not exist. There is no such thing as ____." The sweeper truck moves down my block every day at the same deliberate pace. Its big windows are tinted black. Once I see some Italian guys trailing the thing, a couple of older men in nice suits who hang out at the social club up the block. My nicknames for them are Face and Knuckles and if they are not the Mafioso who are still rumored to run my neighborhood, then I don't know who are. They keep their distance from the sweeper, watching. Is it doing their work? Or is this a move from Providence? Another morning, the hipsters across the way come surging out of their garden apartment, all three with Go-Pros strapped to their heads. They swing onto the sweeper's running boards and tug at its door handles. But of course they don't manage to get inside. The implacable vehicle keeps moving and they cling to it beyond my line of sight.

In time, a few intrepid bloggers claim to have followed these things to their home bases. On the margins of every borough, every neighborhood are warehouses, utility sheds, blank-faced buildings holding out against gentrification. The sweepers are reported to retreat into these. But the photos I've seen on Instagram or in the *Post* are inconclusive: just the tail-ends of big machinery, pulling into garages. Who knows whether these are clues—and if they are, to what? The owners of these alleged buildings have not been found. The phone numbers displayed on the sides of such buildings, features of permanent "for rent" signs, are inevitably disconnected, or have been reassigned. One evening my own phone rings. "What does it mean?" screams a woman on the other end. "I know you know!" What can I tell her but "wrong number"—what the ringleaders themselves would probably say, if someone managed to get ahold of them. Within a week PSAs appear on the subway, reminding us that 911 is for emergencies only.

All the while I build my collection of words, expanding the list to include words of three syllables. *Washington, abortion, perfection, depression.* I'm no longer even sure about that –n. An aural trick, an aura around the spot where a word should be. I keep a legal pad next to my keyboard; I take notes during lulls in my live-chat test-support shifts. Never before have I been quite this regular in my writing practice—and what does that mean?

"Nice words," my co-worker Alexandro tells me, two weeks into the announcements. He's an affable half-Greek kid on the tech support team; the office celebrated his twenty-third birthday with drinks last month at a cheesy Irish pub. Nothing exactly happened between us that night: a lot of joking; some arm- and knee-touching; a kiss on the cheek when my train came first. Since that night he's come by my pod more frequently. Especially as now, when my pod-mates are at lunch.

"Revolution," he reads. He leans against my side-desk. "Education, masturbation, communication. All nice words."

"But not *le mot juste*," I say, hoping that like me he doesn't actually speak French. I know this phrase as the title of a course offered in my MFA program. I should have taken that course. "Sometimes I feel like I'm almost there . . . on the brink of figuring it out." I roll my chair away from the monitor's unflattering glow. I'm six years older than him, already deeply invested in eye creams.

"I think about it in the shower," he tells me. Propped on the side-desk, he push-pulls the base of my chair with his feet. "That's where I go after the truck passes my place. Straight to the shower."

I picture his lanky body, wet. "Tell me more about that part of your process."

"There's some soap, some steam, a lot of rubbing." His feet work my chair slowly.

"And has this yielded any results?"

"Well—those are personal." He stands and drums his long fingers on my legal pad. "We should work on this together."

"Your shower or mine?"

"Definitely yours." He holds my gaze for a moment, shrugs. "But I'm not just a sex object, you know. I've been making recordings, analyzing these messages."

"I'd thought of that, too—that with the right equipment you might be able to hear something."

He shakes his head. "That's not really the result I'm getting. I'd like to show you my data."

"Sure you would."

"Well, I've already seen yours." He biffs my list again. "Are you free later?"

We agree that I will go to his place, after our shifts. I will bring my words, my expertise at word games; I will bring my vocabulary.

"I'll come by for you at five-thirty," he says. Then he drags my roller chair to the middle of the pod and spins it by its arms hand-over-hand, as if it's a merry-go-round. "The spin-off," we call this form of office torture or flirtation, and I fill with heat as I scooch dizzily back to my keyboard. *He's too young*, I tell myself, *he's goofy-looking. He's not a writer.* I slept exclusively with other writers in graduate school and during my first months in New York—men (boys really) who were brilliant, ambitious, unreachable. Here in the city they freelance or edit magazines. They live on nothing and know everyone. I spend forty-five hours a week writing practice tests; I can't keep up with them anymore. Seeing such boys at readings or parties or even on the street always leaves me with a heightened sense of my own peripherality. I look for myself in their stories, find nothing.

There's no such thing as ____, I repeat to myself at 5:30, as I pack up my things. That sentence is my current project and tonight I am doing research toward it. I hold this in mind as Alexandro and I ride the elevator and walk to his car, a battered station wagon stashed at a broken meter. Caught up in his programming, he'd missed his train that morning and driven in from Yonkers. I seldom take cabs in the city and have never ridden through it like this, in the front seat of a regular car. We listen to The Clash on cassette tape and speed up FDR more nimbly than I'd imagined possible. "It doesn't bother you," he asks me, feigning a thick accent, "my Greek driving?" "It doesn't bother you?" he asks again, when he reveals his rented room—one dim chamber in a sub-basement, with a shared kitchen and bath. The last writer I slept with lived in NoHo, in a flat purchased and expensively decorated by his mother. He considered it bourgeois to own books. Alexandro might, too, from the look of things. I tell him the apartment doesn't bother me.

"Have a seat." He offers the only seat, a frayed desk chair. When I sit it rolls freely on the bare linoleum and he catches it by the arms.

"No spin-off." I wrap my ankle around his calf—to stop him, to start something else. But he lets go.

"I'll get us drinks." His dark hair nearly touches the room's dropped ceiling. "Don't open the door to strangers."

Does this imply that we are something else? I roll to Alexandro's desk, pass the mouse across its pad. The two huge monitors wake. Hubble photographs fill the screens, bright and fathomless. *There is no such thing as—*

"For you." He's drinking a High Life but hands me a can of Guinness—what I ordered on his birthday. He takes up the wireless keyboard and sits just behind me, on the edge of his neatly made bed. Everything about the room is tidy, albeit cramped and dingy. Plastic sets of drawers hold his clothes along the room's margins. A stack of USED textbooks serves as a bedside table. (Books, after all). A poster of *The Scream*; a poster of *The Kiss*.

"It's like a dorm room," I say. "I guess that makes sense."

"Four-fifty a month," he says. "Utilities included."

That's less than half my Brooklyn rent. But from the room next door comes a man's anguished grunting, the clang of metal on metal.

"Weights," Alexandro says, typing. "Every night."

"Or a minotaur," I suggest.

"Ah." He feigns the accent again. "You know my people's culture?"

I shrug. "How do you say—" I point to the door.

"Pórta." He gives me the Greek words for desk, chair, floor, ceiling, hand. We are here to share words, after all. I point to the window, the floor, my foot. I point to *The Scream*. I swivel the desk chair toward him, point to *The Kiss*.

"To filí," he says. "Filí mou."

"Feely moo?" I repeat.

"This means 'kiss me,'" he says, still in that ridiculous voice. "Filí mou."

The sounds are unsensual, silly even, but his long torso tapers to his trim waist—and I think of a filmstrip from middle school that illustrated the Pythagorean theorem by tracing triangles on cartoon Greek bodies. I draw the keyboard from his lap and lean toward him and he tugs my chair closer, leaning toward me. His mouth tastes like cheap beer. His mouth tastes like college, this room feels like college, and it is like going back in time when he pulls me from the desk chair and onto his thighs. "Should I get a—" he asks, when our clothes are off. "Yes," I say, and he dives from the bed toward those plastic drawers, searching until he finds a condom. It is like college sex, enthusiastic and a little clumsy, except for the way he watches me with those big eyes—and for the reasons that I close mine.

"Would you have come home with me that night at McGillicuddy's?" he asks, kissing me afterward.

"No." I had gone home after his birthday celebration and written in my notebook, pages barely decipherable the next morning. The final maudlin lines sometimes run through my head: "as if lodged between lives and craving / you." Lines with no definite object—but I am no poet.

"I'm glad you did tonight. But I don't want you to think I brought you back here just to fool around."

There are no pillows on his bed and his Pythagorean chest is hard and hairy beneath my cheek. "Why not?" *What else is possible between us*, I am already thinking. *What am I doing here?*

"Come here." He loops his long arms around my waist and pulls me with him to the foot of the bed. "Look at these."

The left monitor fills with jagged strata: peaks and valleys, drawn in electric colors. "Sound waves?"

"This is a week's worth of messages." He scrolls through, pointing out little differences from day to day, modulations in the sweeper's unvarying message. The differences elude my ear, even when he plays the audio back slowly. "Why are they re-recording this, every time?"

"Maybe someone is actually speaking—it's not a recording after all?"

"No." He shows me the data from a single day: the pattern of waves repeats exactly. "It's just a recorded loop. But you see how each day differs from the days before and after it. A different recording, every day."

"Even the blank is different." Because on the screen I can see it for a blank. Not a murmur, but a gap in the message, silence except for the static of the speakers. These blanks vary in duration.

"So different things must fit in those blanks." He looks at me in the computer light, and though he is much younger than me his deep-set eyes give an impression of wisdom.

"*If* the blanks have meaning at all," I say, remembering the assessment of my neighbor: *PoMo bullshit.* "These variations might just be part of the project—tempting people like you and me to look for meaning where there isn't any."

"Maybe." He kisses me. "But I don't think so. Let's say that we accessed the database of an online dictionary, one with audio pronunciations. And we synced these sweeper recordings to the speed of the dictionary-reader."

"Okay," I say. "But it's not as though words have unique durations. There would still be thousands of words that might fit each of these blanks."

"But we would narrow down the possibilities. A really awesome computer program could do that for us." He types quickly and a list of dates and numbers appears on the other monitor.

"Such as yours already has . . ." I trace his long spine with my fingertips, its curve toward the computer. "Am I here to go through all the eligible words?"

"There's no point," he says. "I mean, at first I thought yes, that would be the next step. But look—" he lunges across his desk, grabs a legal pad like mine. "I wanted someone else to see . . . by the time I finished writing the program, I had six days of recordings. And these are the numbers of possible words that my program originally yielded for each day's blank. I backed everything up on paper."

On the page of his legal pad dated May 6, he's written the durations of the blanks broadcast on May 1, 2, 3, 4, 5 and 6, respectively, along with the numbers of possible words for each of those blanks. In black ink, his numbers are vigorous and clear. The next sheet in the notebook is dated May 7, with data for the dates May 1-7. And so on through May 13, today.

"Now look at how some of the results change. Like this .67 second blank from May 2. See how the number of possibilities for that blank dropped by one digit when I ran the program on May 4, then dropped again on May 10?"

On the screen I see that the May 2 tally is now 37,219 instead of 37,221, as he'd originally recorded: 37,219 possible words instead of 37,221. He watches me glancing back and forth.

"And do you see what else is special about those two dates? The blanks for May 4 and May 10 are also .67 seconds long."

"So the same word fits all three blanks?" I rub my eyes, squinting.

"Well yeah, it could, but we can't realistically determine that: too many possibilities. My point is that every time the recorded blank is .67 long, there's one less eligible word."

"One fewer," I say, reflexively. "Possibilities are countable." This is the stuff of standardized tests; this is familiar.

"Okay." He runs his hand across his face, across the bristle of black stubble coming out along his jaw. "But do you see what I'm saying? Words are disappearing from this tally. Every blank of .67 seconds should yield exactly the same number of possible words: 37,221. Why does the count drop by one digit every time—and why is it dropping retroactively?"

"Your program could have an error," I suggest. "And dictionaries are revised periodically."

"Believe me, I've checked my work. There's nothing wrong with the code. And you can't tell me they revise the dictionary every day."

I look at him in the semi-darkness, a stranger. "So what's your hypothesis?"

He gestures at the analytics he's generated. "It's taking away words. The street sweeper."

My skin prickles, as though somebody walked over my grave. Ridiculous—the suggestion, my reaction. Am I afraid of his theory? Or of a person who would offer this as a valid proposition? I drop back onto the mattress. Big HVAC pipes hang directly over my head. Real pipes, ugly and encroaching. Tangible. I know myself to be too impressed by tangible things. But the theory, the ceiling, the car, the posters, the clanging of metal coming again from next door . . . *what am I doing here?*

"I should go," I tell him. "I work tomorrow, and I'm sure it's going to take a while to get back to Brooklyn."

"Oh." He looks down at me. "I thought you might stay."

"I should go. If you can drop me at the train that'd be great."

"Sure." He turns off the monitors, turns back toward me. His face is dark. "Do I really sound that crazy?"

"It's not that. It's just . . . I haven't been getting much sleep with these messages and everything, and I think it's best if we slow this down. Think it through."

"Sure." He pulls on his t-shirt. "But what if I'm right?"

What if he is right—and I'm just a sour disbeliever, heading home to have my words erased while I sleep? Worst-case scenario: a word a day isn't much. There are so many words that mean practically the same things, so many words we'd never miss. James Joyce used over 30,000 different words in *Ulysses*. More words, possibly, than I'll use in my lifetime. The vocabulary of Agatha Christie's novels shrank by thirty percent in the last twenty years of her life. Computer analysis shows this—I heard about it on NPR. But even without that thirty percent, she could write books. Diminished books, maybe; I can't say. I have never read any of her work (just as I've never read *Ulysses*). I've only heard her story, a story told by computers. Computers can show us what we don't feel, or don't want to: the contracting of our abilities. And I can't seem to write anymore . . . though that started months before the sweeper came.

"This isn't much data," I tell him. "This is correlation, not causation." A logical fallacy that I am paid to practice, in writing wrong answers for fake standardized tests.

"Don't you hate that feeling," he says, looking at me with his owlish eyes, "when you're trying to remember a word and you can't? Such a relief when it comes to you. But what if it didn't?"

"You said you wanted me to bring my list. If a word is missing, how could I have it?"

"You don't," he says. "None of us does."

"Oh, come on." I shake my head. "What if something I wrote down two weeks ago just got swept yesterday? It's still in my notepad, right? Or was I compelled by some *force* to erase it?"

"The brain fills in all kinds of gaps, all the time. You must know that." He sounds exhausted—or disappointed— looking away from me into a dark corner of the room. "If one of the swept words is in your notes, we just can't see it anymore. That's what *I* think."

"Okay." I sit up next to him. "Say I believe you. How is it possible? You think it's some kind of hypnosis, the sweeping? A government conspiracy?"

He wakes up the monitors again. "That's the part I don't understand. I see the effects, not the cause."

"And not the reason."

"There are a million reasons to take away people's words," he says. "And if we don't notice it's happening?"

I shiver again and he puts an arm around me. That searching feeling, the trace of something not quite remembered . . . it's been the hallmark of my existence, these past two weeks. A feeling I wake up to that never quite goes away. I kiss him and we move together again, more solemnly this time. We are searching, he and I, only pretending to be beyond words.

After sex I stare again at that ugly ceiling. "For argument's sake, let's say this is happening. How could we prove it?"

"Besides this?" He gestures toward his data. "Numbers seem like the best proof."

I rub my eyes. "If you can't demonstrate that something is missing, the numbers don't mean anything."

"Well . . ." He props himself on an elbow, strokes my arm. "I have another idea, too. Say I—*we*—went away somewhere—like up into Canada. If we found a place where these messages couldn't reach us, when we came back, we'd be able to see what was missing."

It sounds like a romantic crusade: a writer and a programmer, saving the English language. "Do you know how to camp?"

"Camping is just sleeping outside."

I try to imagine the two of us alone in a tent. Is he a hero or a lunatic? How will we pass the time? "We should bring a lot of books . . . all kinds of books, so that we have as many words as possible shored up for when we come back."

"Or we could just take a bunch of vocab flashcards."

Our company's proprietary cards are filled with words like "mendacious," "risible," "noisome." Are these the words we should be safeguarding? "Refulgent," I say to him. "Nonplussed."

"You're right," he tells me. "I minored in Poly Sci—we should take those books."

I fill a duffel bag with USED copies of de Tocqueville and Studs Terkel while he sets up a recording device in the apartment window. It will upload the sweeper announcements directly to his cloud storage, he tells me: the data will keep coming, the blanks will be recorded and archived, even after we're gone. We pack his station wagon with his big desktop computer, a mildewed tent, and all the food from the shared kitchen, and we drive to Brooklyn to get my things: clothes, skin care products, my unread copy of *Ulysses*. We don't look at the clock as carefully as we might, between these errands and that shower we'd teased each other about. He translates the label of my fancy Greek shower gel: *uplifting, clean and fresh*. I confess that I thought of him when I bought it. Thus we are just fastening our seatbelts again when we hear the sweeper coming. "_____ does not exist," it announces, as it does every morning. The man's voice is commanding but patient. "There is no such thing as _____." Now I know that the gap is powerful, potent. It represents something I don't want to lose. It represents what I've already lost.

"Come on," I urge Alexandro. He fumbles with the key, his long hand seeming to tremble in the faint light. Finally the engine turns over but we are parked in so closely that he will have to inch the car out of the spot.

The city itself is a machine that takes things away—I have learned this much in ten months. It's taken away the energy I had when I moved here, my faith that I am a writer, a faith that was never about having a degree, but grew during the experience of getting it. Those years of school were like being in a big tent with books in the middle of nowhere, unsure whether the other campers were heroes or lunatics. I could be in the tent again, if Alexandro's car would just start, if the two of us could believe in his idea long enough to reach the border, show our passports, find a pine forest without bugs or drunks or other, brighter tents luring us apart. *Stay with me*, I want to say—words that won't come, and not because I've lost them.

The sweeper must be stalled; it isn't advancing. "Look," Alexandro says, shoving open the car's sun roof. I rise through it, swaying as he edges his way out of the spot. Down the street I can see a line of people forming across the sweeper's path: the Mafioso, the hipsters, the Eritrean family that runs the Laundromat.

"People are blocking it," I tell him. "Should we help?"

He puts his hand on my thigh, pulling me down into the passenger seat. "What do you want to do?" The car's front bumper is clear of the parking spot. "Do you want to go with me and figure this thing out—or do you want to stay here and be part of whatever's going on?" He looks stern in the half-light—as well as young, goofy, unlettered.

I think of the mildewed tent staked in the woods, of the two of us sweaty and unshowered, having sex and eating granola bars, isolated from everyone else. How long can we call in sick before we lose our jobs—and how obvious will it be to our coworkers that we're calling in sick *together*? How will I explain myself to my roommate; will she even notice I'm gone? And when we come back, what then? If no one has stopped these sweepers so far, what difference could the two of us make?

I think also of my legal pad, out in the woods, filling up not just with words but with work, as it did when I lived in that other, institutionalized tent in the woods. We could spend our afternoons reading, Alexandro and I; we could finally get to things too long or complicated to read on the subway. And it wouldn't just be self-indulgent, our life in the woods. When we came back . . . when we came back, we would have to find a means of broadcasting our words. We would have to re-educate New York: Thoreau meets sci-fi. No one in the writing world would have noticed my disappearance; how, then, could I expect them to take notice of my reappearance? Did I have it in me to stand with Alexandro and try to speak—knowing that we wouldn't be heard? And that's presuming that Alexandro's program would show us the truth, and that we would return with a truth to speak.

"Are you coming or not?" Alexandro asks. He's fixated on the rearview mirror.

The car promises me one thing and the city another, and if the city has withheld its promise from me so far, on this morning it seems to invite me into it, through the linked arms of my neighbors. I kiss Alexandro and then . . . I want to believe that I do the right thing. As I switch this story now from present tense, with its conceit that all of this is still unfolding, still malleable, into past tense, the only true tense, I would like to believe that I took a risk, made a brave choice that morning when I got out of the car and joined the protest. What I can tell you is that my neighbors' names are John Sciboni and Lester Minkins, and they are not mobsters but a gay couple, both real estate developers. For a week or so I stood with them every morning, my arms linked with theirs, letting the sweeper nudge me down the street. For a month or so after that the hipsters and I chatted on the subway, comparing the fading sweeper bruises on our hips and making abstract plans to see a show or get a drink sometime. Once I even gave a reading with some of my MFA classmates—work inspired by the sweeper. We wrote flash fiction about the sweeper as a social experiment, a government conspiracy, a projection of the collective unconscious. I wrote a prose poem for the occasion, using only words that could be fashioned from the letters of Alexandro's full name, Alexandro Stephen Constanopolous:

She scans her phone: no calls, no texts. A screen as clean as a street. No note under her door, no last letter. No shouts or harsh sex or other upsets—only a deep pull north. He's an axe; she's a spoon. Salt-laden, she spoon-races to the sea. The scoured streets contract and trap. But the sea, that surplus—the sea sounds, ceaselessly. The truth's a red coal that sears her. The sea drenches her, but doesn't put her out. Now she's a corroded spoon, anchored to shore. He showed her a truth that a spoon can't shout: no throat, no sound. She echoes as a shell, alone.

At 108 words, "A Spoon Can't Shout" was the longest piece I'd finished since grad school—and I only broke my constraint three times. No one else was paying attention; no one else could have known what well those letters were drawn from.

In time we all got used to the sweeper's message; it became meaningless. A street evangelist might preach about it; a homeless person rant about it. And sometimes even now when I wake up in the morning I can almost hear the word not said by that calm, emphatic voice. Other mornings I sleep right through it. At work, Alexandro was soon replaced, though I don't know whether news of his termination reached him. Before long there was another gangly kid in his early twenties, occupying Alexandro's place in the tech support pod, solving our customers' problems with the test-taking software. "Send word," I'd said to him that morning, after I kissed him and before I got out of his car. A stupid thing to ask for—the thing most likely to vanish before it reached me. I'd thought I was being playful. Now I remind myself that he could have stood with me that morning, tried one thing before he tried the other. I wish he would have; I think I might have driven away with him after the neighbors unlinked their arms. I think I might have been convinced after that one additional test. Call it a stress test: how much pressure can a human barricade withstand? How much of the problem did we even grasp? But by the time the sweeper nosed through our arms that morning, Alexandro was gone.

inheritance

My boyfriend's mother died and left behind a farm. There was an auction, after he'd come back to the city; all the wrong things were sold. When he found out, he held his head in his hands.

"I have to go back," he said. "I can't fix things from this distance." I said I'd go with him, thinking of a long weekend, thinking I'd be the one who walked with him in the afternoons, helping him cry.

"We don't cry," he told me, two travel days later. We were sitting at his mother's kitchen table. "Not since Kevin died."

"Kevin?" It was the first time I'd heard that name.

"My cousin," said Jarvis. "He died when I was three."

"What happened?" I asked. "I'm sorry."

"Farm accident." Jarvis stood up. "That's all I can tell you."

Jarvis didn't want my help making phone calls, or driving around the four surrounding counties in search of the lost items. He said he'd prefer to be alone.

"Your family doesn't like me," I said, mostly so that he'd correct me.

"No," he said. "You don't understand them."

What I did understand was that he considered me to be different than they were, and that being among his relatives made him like them, impenetrable. Openness was something we were working on, in the city.

"What can I do to help you?" I asked. "I'm here to help."

"Could you look over those chapters in my bag?"

"Nothing else? I'll feel strange just reading."

"Well, imagine how I always felt." And off he went again.

"Are you going to marry Jarvis?" asked his cousin Jenny. She stopped by every afternoon. She was twelve years younger than Jarvis, still in high school. "You don't have to say," Jenny said. "But wouldn't it be weird to marry someone else, now that you've lived with Jarv for so long?"

"I'm not planning to marry anyone," I said. "I don't believe in marriage." This was true: I didn't.

"What does Jarvis think?" She sat across from me at the kitchen table, picking up his papers and putting them down.

I laid my hand flat across my own notebook. "He feels the same way," I said. "Lots of people do."

Jenny smiled. "When people around here don't get married, it's usually that they're lazy or they don't care for each other."

"Well, that's your opinion."

"Not just mine."

"What about you," I asked. "Do you have a boyfriend?"

She shrugged. "The boys here are dumb hicks."

"Is that a yes?"

"Maybe you and Jarv can fix me up when I come visit you." When I didn't respond immediately she laughed. "Don't worry. My mother doesn't like me to be around those that are living in sin."

I couldn't tell whether this was her phrase. "Your mother has a pretty harsh way of putting it."

"Well," said Jenny. "She believes in marriage."

◆ ◆ ◆

His mother's house was situated on a county road, midway between two towns of 300 people each. Though it sat on one hundred acres of farmland, it was not a farmhouse but a one-story ranch. Jarvis hadn't decided yet whether he was going to sell it, and its rooms were strange and half-stripped, possessed of furniture but lacking, he explained, the collectibles that his mother had accumulated in her seven years as a widow. Depression glass, dolls, books bought by the box-load at estate sales and never unpacked. These were the things he'd had auctioned, but with them had been mixed important things, letters and journals and photographs. Things that had already been salvaged once.

The story of this earlier salvation was one of the first he'd told me, back in the story-telling phase of our relationship. A fire had started with a blown fuse, consuming the kitchen while his parents pulled furniture from the other rooms. The house was lost by the time the volunteer fire trucks arrived. Jarvis was six at the time; he remembered afterward the luxury of staying at his aunt's place, which had an oil furnace and an indoor toilet. He described the burned house as drafty and dangerous. Half its rooms were closed off to save on heat and the front porch was halfway caved in. He had a scar under his eye from where he'd gone through a window playing bullfighter with his cousins; the soles of his feet were spotted from stepping on nails loose in the floor. His father had bought the place cheap from the Amish and never gotten around to making updates.

The current house was modern but not convenient. No one had ever bothered to plumb the bathtub, or to wire the basement for electricity. Countertops seemed dirty and wouldn't scrub clean. Not finding pictures of the family, I imagined his parents with pitchforks and thin lips, and Jarvis wearing flour sacks like a child of the Depression. In spite of this, he'd made himself the best-educated person in his family: his own father had barely finished high school, and earlier generations hadn't even gone that far. I was proud of his accomplishment—that, knowing himself to be different, he'd had the courage to act on it. He didn't take well to this comment.

"Different how? From who?" He was fixing the kitchen sink, which whined high and long whenever the cold water was used. I'd failed to hand him a flathead screwdriver; I was sitting at the table again. "Do you have any idea how difficult all of this is?"

"I didn't mean anything against your family. I just meant that I'm proud of you for doing what you wanted."

"I'm too lazy to farm. Too cynical."

This wasn't how he talked about it in the city, if he talked about it at all. "Then you *are* different. I mean in a good way."

"I don't see the sense in sacrificing myself to make a living. A lot of people around here feel the same way. They just can't see a way of getting out."

"You're a good example. For your cousins."

"It's not the same." He rifled through the toolbox. "They're happy here—they have friends. I never did. My parents weren't like my aunts and uncles."

"They didn't let you have *friends?*" This was a new detail.

He grimaced, tightening a knob. "I never had time. Too much to do around here."

I knew that he'd had a lot of chores, growing up. "Look how disciplined you are now. Maybe your parents knew what they were doing."

Jarvis coughed. "My father was cheap. We had to work 14-hour days because he wouldn't update his equipment. He wasn't impressed with modernity—neither of them was."

"That's done with." I stood and touched his back. His t-shirt was damp. "You left."

"Sure." He bent to reopen the sink's shutoff valve. "Try it now."

I lifted the faucet handle and water shot in every direction.

I was alone during the day but never for long. The uncles came by to check on the crops. They were quieter than men I knew of a similar age. When more than one of them was present, they sat together in the living room instead of with me in the kitchen. The aunts gathered around the Formica table and drank the coffee I poured. They brought me magazines that they were done with and videotapes of school events featuring the cousins. I watched Jenny leading the high school dance team, playing her trumpet in a recital, showing her steer at the county fair. She rode the school bus to our stop in the afternoons; she hit rewind when she caught me watching these videos.

"What's FFA?" I asked.

"Future Farmers of America."

"You're kidding," I said.

She pulled the video out of the machine. "It's the same as 4-H, except we can't do 4-H because the pledge is against our religion. I can't believe you'd watch this."

"I liked it."

She threw the tape into her backpack. "How much longer are you staying, anyway?"

"It's up to Jarvis."

"So you're just sitting around until he's ready to leave?"

"It's the least I can do."

"That's true." She shook out her long blond ponytail. "Why didn't you come to Aunt Becky's funeral?"

"Jarvis wanted to come alone. Plus I had to work."

"Did you get fired?"

"I'm taking vacation time."

"You get paid while you're here?"

"Yes."

"That's cool," she said, twisting her hair into a knot. "The reason I asked is that he doesn't seem to pay much attention to you."

How could she begin to assess this, seventeen, having seen us together so seldom? "Is that what everyone thinks?" I said. I said it without raising my voice.

She shrugged, letting her hair fall loose again. "It just seems funny. Coming all this way to sit in a dead person's house. I'd be bored out of my mind."

From below the living room window came a strangled scream. It made me jump; Jenny stood.

"The cats need to be fed," she said.

Those cats! Though the farm animals had been divided up among the uncles, the cats, unwanted, remained—and no matter how much we fed them, there wasn't any relief. They shrieked while fighting and while mating, angry after a month of scavenging. They were skinny orange and white creatures, untouchable and runny-eyed. When I poured out their food on the milk room floor, I could hear hissing in the haymow above me. I'd had cats as pets my whole life, but these made my skin crawl, with their small, glaring faces and their brutalized ears.

"I can get them on my way out," Jenny said. She zipped up her book bag.

I shook my head. "I should get out of the house."

She nodded. "You should."

Jarvis came home one night with a box of letters. They'd been sold to a local historian who demanded twice as much to return them as he'd paid in the first place. This didn't matter.

"They're from my grandfather to my grandmother," Jarvis said. "During the Second World War."

I watched him open the envelopes. His grandfather's handwriting was dark and definite, smudged in places as though he'd passed his hand across the wet ink. There were more recent letters, too, to and from his parents. When I asked about them, he shrugged.

"My mother went to the University of Wisconsin for a year and a half."

"Why didn't she finish?" I lifted the neat bundle.

He took it from me. "She got sick so she came home. Then my father asked her to marry him and she didn't go back."

Jarvis and I had spent the years since our college graduation following each other from graduate programs to job openings. I could understand deferral, but not denial. "Do you think she was happy with that?"

"I don't know—is *your* mother happy?"

I blushed. "I didn't mean it like that. It's only that I can't imagine . . ."

"Don't worry, I wouldn't ask you to stay here." He looked up from the letters. "I might even ask you to leave."

"Oh." I stood up and started toward the kitchen. "I'll call in the morning and check on flights."

"No," he said. "No—don't be like that. I only meant if I needed to stay longer than we'd planned." He followed me, put his arms around me. "Stop," he said. "Things aren't as bad with you here."

I had no way of knowing, either way.

In the strange Central Time Zone that bumped television up an hour, we went to bed early and we went to bed tired. For me, though, the absolute darkness and quiet precluded sleep. The lack of sensation was disorienting and I felt an anxiety I hadn't since childhood that maybe if I fell asleep I wouldn't wake back up. Jarvis slept with his arms wrapped around his chest; on the guest bed that lacked a box spring, I couldn't move without disturbing him.

I lay on my back and stared toward the ceiling, and sometimes a car coming around the bend at the just the right angle would send its headlights as far back as the house. I could hear the difference between trucks, cars and tractors—probably I always would have been able to, but this was the first time I'd bothered to listen and compare. The headlights caught the mirror over the bureau and moved a short ways up and across the ceiling before blinking out; I held my eyes open wide and imagined after-images. When the alarm clock went off the next morning, I saw that there actually were stains spreading across the ceiling.

"You should have the roof checked before winter."

"Oh," he said. "That's not a leak."

"Isn't it?" The blotches were brown and creeping, darker along the edges than in the middle.

"It was a problem up in the crawlspace, a long time ago—I'd almost forgotten. Typical of them to never repaint."

"What kind of problem?"

He shook his head. "Some kind of fire—my dad and I got it out."

"Maybe I should keep an extinguisher under my pillow."

"Mmm," he said. "My father said it was lightning. But what are the chances, right?"

What were the chances? He pulled me with him into the center of the spineless bed, and though I wouldn't have been surprised if he'd felt or acted different in his dead mother's house, things were the same as always, and as always, and with shame, I was grateful to him for loving me.

On Friday there was a tractor pull in town—the last of the season. We went after eating fish fry at the Buck Stop bar. The table was packed with aunts and uncles and cousins because Jarvis's uncle Lee was competing. He'd won three tractor pulls that summer and was drunk by the time his class was announced. We watched him pull a weight sledge behind the tractor; by some mechanics that I didn't understand, more weight dropped the farther the tractor went.

"He's not shifting soon enough," said Jarvis's cousin Matt. "He's going to stall in a minute here."

It was less than a minute in actuality. The tractor gave a lurch and a groan and that was it. It was the least stimulating competitive event I'd ever seen. "The Entertainer" followed Lee's defeat, a tractor with hydraulics and flames shooting out of its exhaust pipes. Roaring up and down the track, it popped wheelies and made a noise that drowned out the demolition derby on the neighboring track. Matt said it competed in professional tractor pulls. I said I couldn't imagine.

We followed the angry sound of the demolition derby to where Jenny stood in a pack of teenagers. She looked more countrified than usual, in her makeup and brash clothes, but she still stood out from the other girls. She put her arm around my waist and introduced me as her cousin.

"Are you drunk yet?" she asked me. "Do you need a beer?" She passed me the bottle she'd been drinking from. Jarvis rolled his eyes and turned to watch the cars fall apart. Jenny wasn't old enough to smoke in public, let alone drink, and I put my hands on her shoulders.

"Hide that," I said. "Somebody's going to see."

"Yeah—who?" She laughed. "I bought this take-out from the bar. Nobody cares as long as you don't drive—and I can't drive anyway."

"DUI," coughed Matt. Jenny drained what was left in her bottle.

"Be careful . . ." I looked to Jarvis, but his back was to us.

"She don't bother to watch her ass because she figures everybody else's already staring at it. Stuck-up," Matt said.

"I am *not.*" She shoved him in the chest, but he didn't even stumble.

"Do you need a ride?" asked Jarvis.

"Troy's got me," she said.

"Troy's up," said one of her girlfriends, and they all ran toward the track, holding each other's arms.

"I thought she didn't have a boyfriend," I said.

"Yeah," Matt said. "She don't have a boyfriend is right."

"Should we do something?" I asked Jarvis.

"You tell me," he said. "What should we do?"

"Take her down and sit on her," Matt said. "That'd be something."

Jarvis spat into the dirt. "Look, she said she's not driving. And neither are you, so don't worry about it."

"How does that make it okay?"

Matt edged between us. "Everything all right here?"

"Fine," Jarvis said. "Nothing another beer can't fix."

Matt put his arms across both our shoulders. "Your round?" And we stumbled back to the Buck Stop bar.

The next morning I was groggy from the cheap beer. I ate crusty Tylenol and waited to feel better. I had spent the end of the night playing darts with Matt and one of the uncles—I didn't know which one. As they overlapped more, I found it more difficult to tell them apart. When I tried to remember Jarvis, later, back at the house, I couldn't remember a thing. He'd left for the day before I woke up.

In the afternoon I went for a walk in the fields, over the fence and across the pasture to where the tall grass ran up against wooded hills. The pasture was strewn with old machinery—broken plows, a combine, a Ford pickup with a wooden bed. There were cars of recent make, too, like a long black Olds with a wasp nest in its trunk. Jarvis had passed his driving test in that car. I wandered through the junk, eating black-cap berries that lingered at the tree line. I'd been warned about bears, so I made noise when I walked into the woods. I'd been told to stand still if a bear charged, to cover my head if it attacked and, if there was any room at all, to run as fast as I could downhill.

But I didn't see anything in the woods, or by the creek, or along the ridge. Divided up like a floor plan, the land was beautiful—but only in the way that people are. I made my way back to the house and found a strange pick-up in the yard.

Jenny was waiting at the kitchen table.

"I thought you couldn't drive."

"I've been driving since I was twelve. Where were you?"

"In the woods."

She looked at my bare legs. "Ever heard of Lyme's Disease?"

"Of course." But I hadn't thought about it at all. I felt a slow kind of panic, the inevitability of a bad thing. "What should I do?"

"Hold still." She stood me under the kitchen light. "Don't look so freaked out—you more likely have wood ticks than deer ticks."

I was relieved to be in the hands of someone who could distinguish between kinds of ticks, but still I felt nervous, with her examining me and the possibility of disease there in the room.

"Better safe than sorry." She pinched the skin behind my ear. "Freckle. How'd you feel this morning?"

"You drank way more than I did." I squirmed as she lifted my hair. "Was that smart?"

"You don't even know." I felt her sigh. "A person could go crazy in a place like this."

"Like what? Tell me." It was easier to ask when I couldn't see her.

"Like . . . anybody driving past knows I'm here because that truck's outside. I mean, they know *I'm* here, because I'm the one out of my family who drives *that* truck. It could make a person crazy. Really, it could."

"I'm not the sort of person who keeps track of trucks." Who was Jenny to complain about privacy? She'd come into the house with no one home. "You should be more careful."

"There's nothing to do around here except church and school and parties." She patted my hair back into place. "Unless you like to write."

"Like Jarvis." Jarvis didn't have his first hang-over until our sophomore year of college. He'd been very serious in high school.

"Sure." Jenny was still behind me. "Or like you."

"What about you?" I turned toward her. "Do you write?"

"Oh, no. I don't even read much." She stepped to the window, scraped her fingernails at the glass.

"Isn't that weird?" I said. "There's tape or something on the other windows, too."

She shrugged. "Things were kind of rushed before the funeral. We were mostly just concerned with clearing them off."

I looked at the window and I could see that it was smudged all over.

Jenny peeled a shred of Scotch tape from the glass. "When Aunt Becky was alive, you couldn't see out with all the paper. Every single window and most of the walls were covered with things she'd written." She looked at me as though I should understand. I shook my head.

"Some of it was reminders," she said. "Like to pick Jarv up from kindergarten. The rest was mostly her ideas. Stuff about how she had to burn the government checks before Uncle John cashed them."

I couldn't tell whether she was joking or not. "Lots of people mistrust the government."

"She thought they were bribing the farmers to grow radioactive corn. She said that's where cancer came from. All she'd eat was organic oatmeal."

I didn't laugh. "She was probably lonely. Lonely people can be paranoid."

"She killed all the chickens because of the corn in their feed. And she took a rifle after the hunters last Thanksgiving. She said orange camouflage meant radiation suits—she said the hunters were government men."

"All that and she wasn't arrested?" I shook my head. "Come on, Jenny."

"Do you see a cop anyplace? She didn't hit anybody. And it's not like somebody's going to press charges against some crazy old widow."

"You shouldn't be saying this." Not about your own aunt.

"If you don't believe me, ask your boyfriend. Ask him about the poison in jet contrails, or the secret messages in barcodes. Ask him who he'd stay with when he came home from college—not her. Anyway, didn't you wonder why he was so worked up about getting her stuff back?"

"He's the executor of the will." But I pictured his face in his hands when he learned of the lost papers. "Were those . . . wall-notes in the auction?"

Jenny shook her head. "We took care of those. But Becky always had a notebook going. Jarvis's old bedroom was just stacked with them. Anybody around here who wound up with one would know exactly where it came from."

"I met her," I said. "I met her at our college graduation, and she was fine."

"Maybe," said Jenny. "But you never met her here."

"I don't know." I remembered Jarvis's mother as a bony hug on graduation day, a woman traveling alone because her husband couldn't get away from the farm. The whole situation had struck me as quaint. How well had I known Jarvis, back then?

"It's not like *she* tried to hide it." Jenny looked at me. "Did he?"

Did he? I looked around the room and saw the other house Jarvis had described, dark and toilsome. He'd told me enough that I should have imagined the rest—or coaxed him into speaking more openly. I had lived in this place for a week without seeing it.

"Thank you," I said to Jenny, "for checking me. Thank you for telling me about this." I put my hand on her elbow. "I'd like to be alone now."

"Are you mad at me? Don't be mad." But she let me guide her toward the front door. "Are you and Jarv coming over for dinner tomorrow, after church?"

"We're leaving in the morning." I hugged her. I hoped this would be true.

Alone again I sat at the kitchen table and listened for trucks turning down the drive. I listened and listened for the sound of an engine but I heard none. No one else came.

I tried to picture what life might really be like, here. In the winter, days would pass without the county plow and nights would shock the furnace still. Spring would arrive late—blanched rainbows, frost at Easter, the smells of manure and exhaust. Then long summer days hot enough to soften asphalt and flies thick on the cows. Crops in the fields, bears in the woods, tractor pulls in town. Fall next, my favorite season. We were on the cusp of it now. I thought of the land ablaze, the harvest coming ripe, and always the feeling of something larger approaching.

That cycle would repeat, year after year. The only thing to change would be her age. The house crumbling because nobody cared for it, the livable space contracting around her. The family would sit around the table, side by side, looking all the same. The men were speechless and the women evaded me. I thought of Jarvis as a child alone, and his father old even when Jarvis was born, and the family drawing around them like a net or a noose against the moment when somebody fell.

When Jarvis came home that evening, the sky was just darkening. I watched him from behind the bared window as he leaned into the trunk of his mother's car and pulled out box after box. I watched him load a wheelbarrow full and push all the boxes in front of him, down behind the chicken coop where the earth was sandy. He didn't see me or wave. He stacked everything together and then he went to the gas tank beside the machine shed and filled a fuel can. From the way he walked, I could tell that he'd filled it full. He threw gas over the boxes and he stepped back. Then there was another fire, and this one didn't come near the house.

the longest night
of the year

Sex. That's all Cameron had really wanted. Uncommitted, internet-facilitated sex and maybe a little conversation. But the woman he brought home—his online date, his supposed match—hasn't emerged from his guest room since she went into it three nights ago, locking the door behind her.

She has access to potable water through the en suite. As far as he can tell, she hasn't taken sustenance of any other kind since their dinner on Friday. She hasn't touched the food he's left outside the door; she hasn't, by all appearances, raided the kitchen while he's been asleep. Not that he's slept much. Over the past sixty-some hours, he's listened to her footfalls, to the toilet flushing, to tinny voices buzzing behind that locked door. The woman hasn't responded to any of his attempts to make contact. "Are you okay?" he's called to her and "I'm sorry." No reply. "I'm tired," she'd said before shutting the door on Friday night. That was the last thing she said to him.

"Isn't this trespassing?" asks Laura, his ex-wife. He phones Laura on Monday morning, once it's become clear that the woman will not be leaving in time for him to get to work. "Or maybe it's one of those vampire situations? You invited her in, and now you're screwed."

Cameron snorts, though he's considered both possibilities. He responds only to the first: "It would be trespassing if I asked her to leave and she didn't."

"Wait," Laura says, "you haven't asked?" Her voice rises to almost the same pitch as their daughters', bright in the background on this, the first real day of winter break. A high school guidance counselor, Laura is off for the week too. "Seriously, Cam? Who is this woman, anyway?"

"I met her online." He's standing in the southeast corner of the dining room, at the farthest point from the guest room. He rests his temples against the two walls. *Like a dunce,* which is precisely how he feels. "You think I deserve this."

"Don't you?" But her tone is gentler. "You brought a total stranger into your home." Laura hadn't wanted the lake house; she'd moved the kids to town after the divorce. Still, he senses the "our" in "your."

"We messaged for a week. She seemed great." At least by comparison. Cameron had recently signed up with three different dating sites. He'd hoped to maximize his prospects, see all the singles who weren't showing themselves in person. So far the local dating scene looked little better online. He matched with women who were too young or too old, with too many kids or pets or lattes in their photos. Women he knew professionally, whose profiles he swiped past, as if looking were tantamount to harassment. But this woman's profile—Theresa's profile— was clean of dependents or prior associations. He might have "liked" her just for that. In photos, Theresa had big, deep-set eyes and long, curly brown hair. A narrow nose and a reserved smile. She was attractive, not hot: someone he could bring without shame to his once-conjugal bed.

Best of all, she would only be in the area through the holidays.

"Which site?" Laura asks. "I want to see."

"She took her profile down. And you'd need an account to view it."

"You think I don't have one?"

"I think I would have noticed you."

"Right."

Cameron pictures Laura rolling her eyes. She's not truly jealous. Her tone is just a reflex, a relic of the days when his outside interests still hurt her. They were together fourteen years, married for twelve; they've been divorced for three.

"I did ask," he says. "I knocked on the door yesterday morning and said it was time for her to leave."

"Then what? She ignored you, so you dropped it." Laura sighs. "Cam, you need to call the cops."

But Cameron does not want that kind of attention: a team of small-town police knocking down the guest room's solid wood door, a gleeful write-up in the thin local newspaper. Whether or not Theresa spoke to a reporter, Cameron would seem culpable. How could he seem otherwise, in a story about his would-be hookup barricading herself in the guest room? He's a financial planner, specializing in estates. It's not in his professional interest to appear culpable.

"It's very Victorian, Cam, having a woman locked in your attic. Maybe that's her thing. Maybe she'll call you Mr. Rochester . . . later."

"I really don't see this leading to a 'later.'" It amazes him now that he ever did. Theresa's manner had unsettled him even during the several hours of their date.

She'd asked to go back to his place the minute she finished her entree. "This scene is so *fake*," she'd said, wadding her napkin between her long hands. "I can hardly breathe with all of the *effort* going on." Her angular face did look a little clammy in the restaurant's low light. "I mean, give it a rest with all the striving yuppie bullshit."

"Of course," he'd said, though he admired the Scandinavian simplicity of the restaurant: blond wood and white linens, walls of windows facing Lake Michigan. Maybe Theresa was objecting to the obscure and self-righteous language of the menu, all the local sourcing and fancy words for bacon. Fair enough—but if this ambience struck her as phony, what would she think of his place? He'd bought a couple of bottles of wine and some good chocolate; he'd stacked a big pile of birch logs by the fireplace and arranged white column candles on the mantle and coffee table. Would she scorn these obvious efforts?

"Do you want to follow me back?"

"How far? I *should* be okay to drive." She'd only drunk one glass of wine. Theresa was thinner than he'd expected, but surely no grown woman could be incapacitated by one drink consumed with a full meal. Unless Theresa wasn't supposed to be drinking at all. Maybe she was on medication; maybe she couldn't metabolize alcohol. But whatever the risks of her driving, Cameron didn't want her to leave her car in a parking lot fifteen miles from his house. He wanted her to be able to leave on her own—even then, before he'd grasped that she wasn't going to go.

"Laura, how am I supposed to have Christmas Eve over here tomorrow if this person is still holed up in the guest room?"

"I can do it," Laura says. "If you're still having this problem at, say, noon tomorrow, give me a call and I'll host. But you have to make the piggy pudding."

"I *can't* make the piggy pudding." He beats his forehead lightly against the dining room walls. Last year's leftover figs and dates are no doubt withering somewhere in his pantry, but he has none of the fresh ingredients at hand, not for that or for any of the other holiday foods the girls will expect. *We WON'T go until we get some,* he hears them singing, loud and off-key. His head throbs. "If I'm still having this problem tomorrow, I won't be able to leave the goddamned house!"

"Maybe *she's* the Mr. Rochester of this situation," says Laura, slowly. "*She* could leave and you can't. It's genius, really—though I can't imagine why anyone would want to keep you captive."

"I'm not *captive.*" But he hasn't even run the snow-blower since Saturday morning, when he'd cleared the drive and scraped Theresa's car, then sat at the kitchen island until midafternoon reheating coffee. "Theresa?" he'd finally called, knocking lightly on the guest room door. In response she turned up the volume of her music. "Theresa? Can we talk?" She hadn't answered, then or any time subsequently.

"I could come over," Laura says. "Play the angry wife?"

"I already told her we're divorced."

"And when I appear, she'll see that you were lying."

"I wouldn't lie about that." He never had. Back when they were married, he'd always mentioned Laura up front. "I love my wife, but I need more," he'd explained, twice to women in similar predicaments and once, disastrously, to someone unattached and searching. He'd learned then about the importance of establishing clear boundaries. Yet here he is, involved in a situation that he doesn't understand and can't resolve. He's scheduled to have the girls from the twenty-sixth until the second. If Theresa is still in the house on Christmas Day, he'll have no choice but to call the police.

"I'll call you back if I need you," he tells Laura. "I'd rather not involve you in this."

"Tell her to get out," Laura says. "Be firm for once, Cam."

He nods at the phone: firm. There's a big difference between firm and threatening—that's important to remember. The idea of again frightening or threatening Theresa disgusts him. But firmness seems possible. Up there alone in the guest room, Theresa must know that she's behaving strangely; she's probably embarrassed. What justification could she possibly offer, after three nights and two days of hiding? His firmness will probably be a relief to her. It's probably what she wants. *No—don't even think "what she wants." Do not for a second think "She wants it."* Cameron pauses in the kitchen, wipes his sweating palms on a dish towel. The woman upstairs is no longer a romantic prospect. The woman upstairs is a trespasser. *It's time for you to leave,* he must make himself say to her. *I've been patient, but I can't have you here any longer.*

"I came up for the holiday," Theresa had told him over dinner, just as she'd said in her messages.

"You have family up here?"

"It's a good place to be right now." She stared out the window, toward the dark bay and the lights curving along its shore. She was dressed in a style that Laura called "middle-aged dishabille": a straight, blackish-green tunic over black leggings; a spidery black scarf looped around her neck; dark stone earrings and lots of silver rings. She told him that she worked in arts administration downstate.

"Well, the ski resorts are happy this year." Cameron took a bite of his grass-fed, organic steak. Theresa had ordered the same thing and was eating it quickly. "Do you ski?"

"I suppose you do?" She raised an arched eyebrow.

"Mostly cross-country." He actually preferred downhill but felt embarrassed to say so. "I could show you some trails later this week."

"I need to go to the woods," she said. She crossed her fork and steak knife on her bare plate. "Can we go now?"

Cam had asked for a doggie bag along with the check; he'd finish his meal later. Despite her odd remarks, her arrogance (or maybe because of these things) he'd still believed Theresa was eager to sleep with him. He'd thought this as he paid the bill, and he continued to think it, driving more slowly than usual so he wouldn't lose her or overtax her winter driving skills on the way out to the lake house. Other women had admired the home's modern lines, but it was obvious to Cameron that Theresa would not. If she liked anything at all about his home, it would be the tall pines surrounding the house and the small inland lake behind it. At least he hadn't yet decorated the yard with white lights and nodding grapevine reindeer for his daughters. The homes he led Theresa past had such trimmings already in place, plus bright, fat trees in their front windows. Beneath those trees, kids were shaking their presents. *Striving yuppie bullshit.* He shivered atop his heated car seat. Would sex with Theresa be a disaster—or a revelation?

Cameron stands now by the coat cubbies, his call to Laura ended, his messages checked, his phone no help at all. He listens for movement above. The guest suite is over the garage, an addition to the original house, with its own set of stairs descending to the mudroom. He climbs those stairs slowly, keeping to the edge, so they won't creak. Reaching the top step, he leans forward and presses his ear to the door. Nothing. Maybe Theresa is asleep. Or maybe she's dead. She's dead because he didn't have the nerve to open the door and check on her.

He has the key in his pocket; he has the key in his hand— and then the sound of running water breaks the silence. The cataract flow of the soaking tub. That giant tub had been Laura's idea. Her parents and sisters were the ones most likely to make extended visits; it had been a nice idea. Then the floor beneath the tub needed to be reinforced, which was less nice. The addition project had been stressful and expensive, another strain on their sagging marriage, and the finished suite eventually served as Laura's bedroom, during those months when they were deciding what to do. Cameron can't recall an invited guest ever actually staying there.

Now Theresa is drawing herself a bath. A relaxing soak, when he hasn't dared to shower since Friday. (Then: a postgym, predate shower; a shower enlivened by mundane sexual fantasies. Hard to imagine, now). But *not everything's about you, Cam,* and maybe Theresa's bath is not intended as an affront. Maybe she's freshening up, preparing to leave. Either way, interrupting her would seem intrusive. It would set an antagonistic tone for their interaction. And a bath offers as viable a timeline as any: he can wait until he hears the tub draining, then wait fifteen minutes more, so she can dress. And then . . . then he'll come back upstairs and ask her to leave. He's entitled to do that, at least.

"Can I take your coat?" he'd offered on Friday night, once they were inside the house. They'd removed their boots in the mudroom, together, and she'd pulled a pair of felted wool slippers from her giant handbag. He couldn't decide whether this was endearing or overly familiar; he had friends who carried house shoes in the winter—but those were not friends he planned to sleep with. Theresa's slippers were dark gray with big red poppies on top. *Poppies: Georgia O'Keeffe: vaginas.* Encouraged, he'd stepped behind her so she could shrug her long coat into his hands. "What is this?" he asked, stroking the kinked fabric of its sleeves.

She moved away, pulling the coat closer to her neck. "Persian lamb."

"It's lovely." He extended his arms. "May I hang it up for you?"

"It's the fur of fetal lambs," she said. "I'll keep it on, thanks."

She'd shown herself into the kitchen and from there into the open dining and living rooms. The moon was full enough to brighten everything. It cast a long trail on the frozen lake, and Theresa crossed directly to the big windows, taking it in.

Cameron didn't follow her, pausing instead at the wine rack, then at the stereo to cue up Miles Davis. There in his home, Theresa reminded him of an advisee that Laura used to bring over sometimes, a troubled tenth-grader. That young woman had worn black lipstick and all the other Goth accouterments, but she loved to play Barbies with their daughters. Not as a babysitter—Laura didn't quite trust her for that—but almost like another sister, who dressed the dolls and moved them in mincing hops through the Dream House, as his daughters did. Whenever Cameron came in earshot, that girl's Barbie went silent; if they had meals together, she answered his questions reluctantly and with scorn. "Daddy issues?" Cameron had asked Laura, after the first labored evening. "Everything issues," Laura said. "She needs a space where she can just stop performing for a while." And he'd felt ashamed of his comment—ashamed that he couldn't help Laura make the kind of space a kid like that needed. "Just hang back when she's here," Laura suggested. "Be receptive, not pushy. Let *her* make overtures—or not." In time the girl stopped cringing at his voice.

"I'll light a fire," he called to Theresa. "Warm things up."

"I'll do it." By the time he'd found a corkscrew, she'd already kindled the logs. The small flames leaped, blue and green, smelling sharply of pine. Theresa sat on the wide bench of the hearth, feeding the fire. When he drew nearer he saw that her eyes were closed, her lips moving.

"Wine?" he asked, too loudly. He clinked the two glasses he held.

"Of course," she answered, blinking. Smiling? He opened the Merlot at the coffee table, so she wouldn't see him struggle with the dollar-store corkscrew. (The expensive, levered corkscrew had moved to town with Laura). He brought the bottle to the hearth and poured Theresa a taste. She took it like a shot, nodded.

"Cheers," he said, after pouring two big glasses. Theresa met his gaze, and he took heart. Not making eye contact during a toast brought seven years' bad luck in bed. Making eye contact therefore meant—

"To new beginnings."

"To the goddess," Theresa said. She took a big gulp of wine, then another, and dashed the dregs of her glass onto the fire.

Cameron did the same. "To the goddess!" He sat down beside her. "Which goddess?" he asked. "You?"

She stood up, swaying. "Where's the bathroom?"

He pointed her to the powder room off the front entry. While she was gone, he refilled their wineglasses, lit the candles, arranged the fancy chocolate on a nice plate. At least one of the candles smelled like vanilla, heavy and sweet. Possibly—hopefully—an aphrodisiac. Cameron rubbed his stockinged feet across the rug and saw bright sparks.

Theresa returned wearing her boots, her coat buttoned. "Are you ready?"

He stood to meet her. "For what?" He held out her wineglass.

"To go to the woods."

"Now?" He let his fingers brush her knuckles as she took the wine. "Look how nice this fire is. Can't we take a walk later?" Theresa didn't answer. But he placed his hand lightly on her forearm, and when he sat down again on the hearth, she sat with him. He offered her the chocolate, and she chose a square.

"Your earrings are lovely," Cameron said. The dark stones caught the firelight.

"Star sapphires." She licked her fingertips clean, then unfastened an earring and dropped it into his palm. "For healing and protection."

The stone was warm from her skin. When he turned it, he saw the star flash inside, a pale asterisk. "Does it work?" He leaned toward her.

"Depends on your energy." She let him slide the earring's post into her lobe, then push the backing into place. She let him bring his face close to hers—but she drew away before his lips made contact.

He sat back, sweating. "Hot fire." He pulled off his sweater, hoping that his button-down wasn't damp at the armpits. "Tell me more about yourself."

"Like what?" Her eyes narrowed above her wineglass. "Do I like to travel? What's my favorite book? What are my unrealized *dreams*?"

"Sure." He was still sweating. "Or whatever."

"You read my profile." Theresa's glass was empty again. "Do we need to go over all of that?"

"No." He smiled. "We don't even have to talk." He reached for her knee, but she shifted away. Maybe she wanted something else. "I would so like to touch you," he said. The wine, the candles, the hot fire blazing—"Don't you want to touch me?" He began to unbutton his shirt, holding her gaze again. He was in good shape for a guy his age; his trainer said so, and other women had, too. But Theresa just watched him with her big eyes, her mouth a wine-stained slash. When he got to his cuffs, she stood.

"I can't drive." She brandished her emptied wineglass. "Where can I stay?"

"Isn't that obvious?" Standing, he caught her hand and drew it toward his ribs. He wrapped his other arm around her waist. He wanted her to feel him, feel how badly he wanted her. He thought that's what they were doing. But she pushed him.

"No." Her eyes moved over his bare torso, and she shook her head. "No."

"No?" He reached for her again, caught her wrists in his hands. "Then why'd you come home with me?" He pulled her toward him, aiming his mouth for the unscarved strip of her neck.

"No!" She stomped her foot, crushing his toes with her boot. He let go, and she jumped to the coffee table. "Stop!" She gripped the cheap corkscrew like a weapon.

He tried to smile. "Seriously?" His toes smarted, but her pose was ridiculous. Had her profile mentioned rough play? "I could take that from you without even trying. I could f—"

"Stop it!" she shrieked. She jabbed the corkscrew in his direction. Her eyes were watering. Her chest was quaking.

"Oh, no." Cameron's stomach clenched. "No, no—I didn't mean—"

"Stop it," she said again, as if she was choking.

"Theresa, you're fine. Everything's fine. I'm sorry." He sat down heavily on the hearth. "I'm sorry. I misunderstood."

Theresa backed away until she hit the sofa, facing him, then dropped onto it. "I need to lie down," she said.

"Okay. That's fine. Just lie down." She was still clutching the corkscrew. "Or—maybe you'd rather go up to the guest room?" And she'd nodded, then followed him at a distance with the corkscrew and her giant handbag. "This wasn't what I expected," he said, after putting clean sheets on the bed and setting out towels, giving her the Wi-Fi password and showing her where the bath salts were—all while apologizing again and again. "Based on everything I've heard about online dating, I thought sex was a given. I shouldn't have—I'm so sorry."

"I'm tired," she said and closed the door. He heard the lock turn; he went to his own room. He brushed his teeth, spitting pink foam into the sink. He threw his sweaty shirt into the hamper.

Am I a rapist? he lay awake wondering all that night. It was cold in the master suite, as it always was after they used the fireplace. The chimney sucked all the warm air out of the house. Cameron shivered. He didn't think he was a rapist. He'd assumed Theresa wanted sex. They weren't kids; they both knew how things worked. It was fine for colleges to revise the rules of courtship—it was great. As a father of girls, he liked the idea that boys would have to obtain his daughters' clear consent. Or girls would, he supposed. Or—and/or— his girls would gain the permissions of whomever they hoped to bed. But he and Theresa were long past college, grandfathered into the old rules. Surely a woman in her forties could be expected to read established signals. Theresa had asked to come home with him. In their shared language, didn't that mean one thing?

"She was asking for it," he said, into the darkness. It sounded even worse out loud.

Am I a rapist? he thought every time he dozed that night and woke up. Not lately, of course, no question about the willingness of his partners during and after his marriage. How many women had he been with, before Laura? Six girlfriends; ten or so hook-ups probably. He tried to count them, to conjure them, to make sure he hadn't screwed up. But he kept drifting from those hazy memories into half-dreams. A bonfire, like back in high school; a girl he couldn't quite see. The hot slipperiness of her—God, how he missed that. Everybody around them all up to the same thing, and he'd managed to get the tip in. *Please*, he was saying, or she was saying, and then his wife was beside them. *Again?* she said. *We're divorced*, he pleaded. *Aren't we?*

The girl ground herself against him, moaning, and he tried to push her away. *No*, he said, *No. You should've asked first*, his dream-wife whispered in his ear, but she was rubbing up against him too. He felt a stirring in his midsection and made it to the toilet just in time to vomit.

Soaking tubs encourage long baths. Cameron tells himself this as he rummages around his garage, beneath the silent water pipes of the guest suite. Theresa filled the tub forty minutes ago. *Long baths are the purpose of soaking tubs.* Maybe he'll take a bath himself, later, once his tub is finally free. In the meantime, the minutes will pass more quickly if he occupies them. He has plenty of tasks to accomplish before Christmas Eve dinner tomorrow night.

The indoor Christmas decorations are inaccessible, stashed in the guest-room eaves. But the yard ornaments are right here, on the top shelf of the garage storage rack. Standing on tiptoe, he topples down the musty boxes of the grapevine reindeer. He unpacks the doe, the six-point buck, two thigh-high creatures prickled with white lights. Tucking them beneath his arms, he tramps across the drifted yard. Every year they stand just outside the dining room windows, lighting up at dusk. His daughters have names for the reindeer; his daughters have posed in countless photos beside these things and will pose in the coming days for more. He buries the long tails of the electrical cords, sets the timer, and plugs it into the covered outlet.

The driveway needs to be cleared again if he expects Theresa's little hatchback to make it out. It'll be at least a twenty-minute job, but it's better than her getting stuck or hung up on the berm of ice the plow leaves at the base of the drive. Back in the garage, he primes and pumps and pull-starts the snowblower. The motor's loud pops must echo off the tub; hearing them, perhaps Theresa will grasp that it's time to go.

He pushes the machine down the long drive, craning his neck now and then to keep an eye on the house, then pushes his way back. When he's made four passes, a lane more than wide enough for Theresa's car, he brushes the snow from its windows. Of course she's not huddled, frozen, inside the car—and he ought not to feel disappointed by this fact.

Cameron sheds his snowy outer layers in the mudroom, then once again climbs the stairs to the guest room. He knocks on the door, firmly. "Theresa, I'm coming in." No answer. This time, he unlocks it.

"She's gone." He speed-dials Laura. "All of her stuff is still here." The big bag is slumped by the bed. The poppy slippers are in the bathroom, beside the spa tub. A ring of twiggy foam shows how high it was filled, earlier, almost to the top. Did Theresa disappear down the drain? "She didn't come down the stairs." Or hadn't while he was in the house. He touches one of the candles on the tub's rim. Its glass is still faintly warm.

"Look out the window," says Laura wearily. And he sees tracks in the deep snow. Theresa didn't jump; she appears to have gone out the back door. Her tracks lead toward the frozen lake, then out of sight, following the shore.

"I've got to go," he tells Laura. "Thanks."

Cameron gathers Theresa's slippers, the laptop and cord resting on the unmade bed. What else? Her rings, sitting in a dish on the bedside table. A pair of black underwear and some sort of bra-type top, both damp and hanging to dry in the stall shower. A phone charger. He shoves all of it into her big leather bag and runs down the stairs, through the mudroom and kitchen, to the living room. Locks the French doors leading to the back deck; checks the matching doors off the dining area. Locks the mudroom, for good measure, though the garage door is down. He pushes his feet into his damp boots and rushes out the front door to Theresa's car.

Locked! Deep in her giant bag, keys clank but don't surface when he shakes the thing and gropes around. Finally he overturns the bag on the packed snow beside her car. Clicks open the doors, shoves Kleenex and tampons, wallet and make-up pouch, notebook and receipts, frozen underwear and everything else into the bag and drops it on the passenger's seat. He runs back to the house, double-locks the front door. What else? He is climbing up from the basement, where the walk-out door was of course already secure, when he hears the dining room doors shaking. Something is trying to get in. *She's* trying to get in. Is it cowardly to wait behind the partial wall that separates the kitchen from the rest of the first floor? (Thank God he and Laura ran out of money and matrimonial goodwill before opening up the floorplan!) Is it cowardly to shift positions as he imagines Theresa circling the house? Looking in through all the big windows, trying to make contact.

I got her out, he texts Laura.

☺, she responds immediately.

Then, the doorbell. Cameron used to tell his daughters they'd break the doorbell if they held it down. Apparently this isn't true. Theresa is on his doorstep, pushing steadily. Outside, but not leaving. Why not?

Crouched beside the refrigerator, he opens his dating apps, pulls up his carefully wrought profiles. His half-smiling face, his irreproachable interests, his bare chest in a beach shot on the raciest site. Looking for: short-term dating, casual dating, casual sex. What did he do wrong? Would the night have progressed normally if he'd agreed to take a walk? He wishes himself back to that moment when he could have risen from the hearth and geared up for the snow. Led Theresa laughing through the deep drifts to the lake—and then what? Made snow angels, savored the stillness. Kissed her under the cold moon.

Now, if he times his breathing to the rise-fall of the doorbell, its blare is almost bearable. Ding-dong. In-out. *Good job*, Laura texts. Ding-dong. Ding-

"I put your purse in your car," Cameron yells, facing Theresa through the front door's three descending rectangular windows. "Purse." He points. "Car!"

She continues to press the bell, staring at him. She's wearing her long fetus coat, its hem white with snow, and her tall boots. She's wrapped her spider-scarf around her ears and mouth. Her pink gloves belong to one of his girls— picked up, probably, as she passed through the mudroom.

"You need to go," he says. "Or I'll call the police."

Theresa pulls the scarf away from her mouth. Her star earrings gleam, for protection. But her face seems thinner than it did Friday night, her big eyes more sunken. She may have eaten nothing in the past three days. How can she possibly be fit to drive? "Let me in," she mouths at him. The doorbell sticks, suspended on the first note.

"No." He shakes his head. "I'm sorry."

She kicks the door, hard. "Let me in."

"Sorry," he says. "I cleared the drive for you."

She turns away, keeping a finger on the doorbell. When she turns toward him again, her coat is unbuttoned. "Let me in," she mouths, drawing the lapel open with her free hand. Beneath the coat, above her boots, Theresa is naked.

Cameron closes his eyes, his ears thrumming with blood. His groin buzzing. Or his phone. *All good for tomorrow?* Laura has texted. He swipes that message aside, turns the screen to show Theresa that he's dialing 9-1-1.

She hits the door with her palm and her coat shifts back on her shoulders. He can see most of her body, pale against the coat's dark satin lining. Pale and toned, as had been impossible to gauge beneath her shapeless outfit Friday night. Her breasts are full, her nipples erect in the cold.

Her pubic hair is trimmed to a narrow dark strip. He lowers the phone, shakes his head.

"You need to go," he tells her. "Go!"

"Fuck me," Theresa's mouth seems to say. He can hear nothing over the doorbell. In his hand, another new message from his ex-wife; on the other side of the door, this trespassing woman. His date, his match, now propositioning him.

Ready for adventure, he'd described himself online. He'd imagined parasailing, couples massage, hot-oil fondue. He had not imagined his home under occupation or the occupier changing tactics so suddenly.

"Fuck me," Theresa mouths again, and it would be like the date starting over, his opening the door to her now. Inviting her in as though for the first time but bypassing candles and chocolate. He'd misread the situation on Friday night. There can be no misinterpretation of the signals Theresa is sending now, with her flesh bared beneath that open coat. She's changed her mind. She's ready—for what, he can only imagine. And will be doomed to only imagine, if he doesn't open the door.

If he doesn't open the door, his already months-long dry spell will extend past New Year's, a holiday he will observe by falling asleep alone while his daughters and a clutch of their closest friends count down the ball drop in the basement rec room. Could he pay the older one to babysit, test his luck with another date? Someone less risky, a friend of a friend? No. Laura had been furious the one time he'd proposed such a plan, and not because she considered the girls too young to stay home alone. "You have them six days a month," she'd chided. "You can't plan around that?"

Well, he'd tried this time—and he'd failed. But if he opens the door now, surely he will succeed, at least in the most primal way. Theresa's cheeks are pink with cold; she can't keep flashing him and ringing the doorbell forever.

"Go away," he tells her. His fingers grip the doorknob. He could open the door. He could pull Theresa into the foyer, fuck her, and push her back outside. And that would be okay, wouldn't it, under these particular circumstances? That might even be what she wants. What does he want?

"In your car," he shouts at the window. "Let's fuck in your car."

She blinks at him, then lifts her finger from the doorbell. "What?"

He cracks the door open—carefully, carefully—and puts his mouth to the gap. "I'll f—have sex with you in your car. If you want."

A long shudder passes over her. "Cloth-ing," she says, over-enunciating. Somehow her mouth makes the same shapes as before. "Upstairs. In the closet. I'm not leaving without my clothes."

"Oh." Cloth-ing. "Right."

Cameron shuts the door, locks it. He avoids Theresa's gaze through the glass. He misunderstood, again. His whole body misunderstood. "Fuck me . . . cloth-ing." Up in the guest suite, in the bathroom mirror, he sees all the differences his mouth makes. He splashes his hot face with cold water.

This time, he'll be more careful. He will not let Theresa mislead him. Nor will he let her send him back endlessly for items secreted throughout the suite. He opens the dresser drawers, the bathroom vanity, the medicine cabinet; he drops to his belly and crawls beneath the bedskirt. He finds only her black outfit hanging, still damp, in the closet. He should've seen it the first time. Although—what kind of person takes a walk in late December, in the nude?

But if she'd been waiting for him to leave the house, what choice did she have? The snowblower had started, and she'd sneaked out the back door. If she'd returned to the house five minutes sooner, he would never have known she'd left. He would have unlocked the door to the guest room and found her there, naked, in the bath or the bed. And what would he have assumed then? What would he have done?

"I'm sorry," he says, as he cracks the door again and passes her tunic and leggings to her. "I already put everything else in your car."

She's buttoned up the long coat, rearranged the scarf around her ears and nose. She is a pair of deep brown eyes, judging him.

"Could you give me back those gloves?" he asks. "They're my daughter's."

Theresa peels them off and lets them fall at her feet.

"Thanks," he says, drawing the door closed. "Safe travels."

He turns the two locks and watches as she walks to her car. Beside the passenger door, she stoops to pick up something from the ground. Some detritus from her overturned bag, his fault, and he sees her glance back at him balefully through the dusk. Her car starts without trouble—a miracle!—but she keeps it in park. Letting the engine warm up and herself, too. He hopes it's not cold enough for frostbite.

He checks Laura's latest message. *Not a vampire,* Laura texts. *She's a witch!* Attached is a link about the Winter Solstice, pagan practices. He skims the article, starting again to sweat. Purification, purging, meditation—is this what Theresa was doing while he fretted downstairs? Was she casting spells? Setting *intentions?* Cameron is not religious or even "spiritual," in the parlance of dating sites. But that doesn't mean he's receptive to new-age witchery. Had Theresa disclosed any of this in her deleted profile?

Inside the hatchback, he sees Theresa's arms rise, stretching, as she dresses. What was she doing, naked in the woods, alone? Cameron's breath fogs the window; he wipes it clear. Theresa arches her back, writhing into her many layers. She straps on her seatbelt, and he watches as she makes a multipoint turn, edging onto the uncleared half of the parking pad. Finally the hatchback is headed down the drive.

Then Theresa pauses, looking toward the house. She taps her horn. Goodbye? No—she's gesturing. Beckoning him.

Cameron opens the front door and steps cautiously onto the porch. Home base, in his daughters' games of tag. On summer nights they throw themselves against the screen door, screaming *Safe!* and *Not it!* Theresa isn't going to spring from her car and race him back here. And even if she did, if somehow she locked him out of his own home, he could unearth the imitation rock that holds the spare key. He could drive her car to town for help, if he had to.

He follows the shoveled path to the driveway, maintaining eye contact with Theresa as best he can in the falling light. The pines are already black spikes against a purple sky. When he reaches the driver's side door, she rolls down her window.

"Here." She extends her arm. In her palm is an oval stone, mottled pink and green. "This was on the ground."

"Sorry," he says. "It must have fallen out of your purse when I put your stuff in the car."

"It picked you," she says. "Take it."

He does. The stone is rough and cool, bright patches of color against veins of darker green. "What is it?"

"Unakite." She looks up at him, fish-eyed. "For emotional issues. It aids spiritual growth and self-awareness."

Which of them has emotional issues? Before he has a chance to object, Theresa has rolled up her window. She touches her fingertips to the center of her forehead, as if she's holding the stone there. Then she hits the gas.

"Hey!" he yells—but the little car is already trundling down the long drive.

Cameron weighs the thing warming in his palm. He deserves an apology, not a pet rock. He deserves a rent check for the past three days, plus other damages, too. He pulls back his arm, sighting the rusted body of Theresa's car. He steps forward, releases.

The stone connects with a crack and ricochets into the snowbank. Theresa brakes, then accelerates, her tires spurting snow. She reaches the road and turns from view. Gone.

The date is finally over. That magic stone didn't even mark the snow.

Beside the house, the timer clicks; the grapevine reindeer raise their heads. Cameron clenches his empty fist. *Safe.* His deer begin to nod, first one and then the other.

apnea

One night in a bar, catching up after years, my friend P. told me the story of how his roommate had died—in their house, in his sleep. By the time P. found out, the ambulance was gone and the police had left. A line of yellow caution tape hung across the doorway of the dead man's room. Beyond that, P. could see that the man's mattress had been removed, and even the carpeting on which the mattress had rested. The dead man had been an ascetic, P. said; the room hardly looked different, and yet it was. The line of weedy plants in front of the bare window, the stacks of library books on the floor . . . nobody was coming back for them.

My friend P. stood outside the police tape and tried to remember when he'd last seen his roommate alive. P. had been spending a lot of time with a girl, a painter who looked like a kindergarten teacher (I'd seen a photo online). In reality, the girl taught line drawing at several community colleges. The dead man had introduced them. An artist's model, he had once posed naked in front of P.'s future-girlfriend and her students. The girl had initially struck P. as *nice*: a sweet, smiling person with brown eyes and bangs, so benign as to seem banal. But he was startled by her paintings when he went with the dead man to her gallery show. The dead man had sipped from a glass of water while P. talked to the girl about her art, and his own. I imagine P. might have told her about how scientists can engineer tomatoes into squares for easy shipping, as he had told me once in a similar situation. P. is always pushing conversations toward what is sinister or wonderful about the everyday. I imagine he might have hunched his shoulders a little while talking to that girl and shuffled his feet. P. has a smile that can seem foxy, when you don't know him well, and then, later, when you do.

It is possible that, standing outside the police tape that morning, P. was able to grasp at once the enormity of what had happened to his housemate. P. has a profound mind, which he cultivates through frequent use of marijuana and occasional use of psychedelics. He says, though, that he stood there for a long while. He was looking for the first time at a crime scene: instead of a body sketched in chalk, here was something more abstract. He did not know then that the police had ripped up the carpeting to run toxicity tests; he could not account for the bare rectangle on the floor. From the doorway he moved in and out of that new, blank space.

P. found his other roommates, two women, weeping in the kitchen. When he came into the room they stared at him as though he had died, too. What could he say to them? He saw that they wanted something. They had called him at his girlfriend's number and told him about the death. They had spent the entire morning calling people, and still they hadn't found anyone who knew the dead man's next of kin. He was—he had been—significantly older than P. and the other roommates. He had been a quiet person who took less than he gave. An exemplar, in their eyes.

Something had happened—with his brain? with his heart? And now the landlord wanted to know what was going on, what kind of drugs they were using or making in his house. The landlord had already been there to see the ruined carpeting, the scars the police had made in the floorboards below. The landlord had stood in the kitchen and said that they had thirty days, and that he was sorry.

Sitting at the table with the women, P. considered where he would go next. Later, he would have time to be dismayed by this reaction—that when face-to-face with his friend's mortality, he was more concerned with his own well-being. But in the moment, it seemed to him like the more pressing issue. P. knew almost right away that, if she would let him, he would go to the girl. And he felt nearly sure that she *would* let him. Living with her, he would find out where her paintings came from, find the part of her that was the very opposite of her freckles and upturned nose. He would cleave through to the core of her. And I remembered, sitting there in the bar, what had happened when we were younger, and he had wanted that from me; how I had lain, paralyzed, for long, long minutes in the dark, because I couldn't explain myself to him or to anyone.

P. is good at waiting, patient—even if he couldn't wait me out. He is a keen observer, as is clear from his own art. That morning in the kitchen he felt himself on the cusp of something, related to life or death or both, and he walked out of that claptrap house into the cornfield behind it, and it wasn't until evening that he went back. The women had gone somewhere, and he felt himself in communication only with the dead man as he folded his t-shirts into a milk crate. He was ready to leave.

The police eventually determined that there was nothing in the carpeting, nothing in the mattress to clarify what had happened to P.'s roommate. Apparently the man had just stopped breathing in his sleep and that was that. The same thing frequently happens to me, though not yet with the same consequences. I wake up, or part of me does, and I can't breathe, and I can't open my eyes. It takes a lot of concentration in these moments to take another running start at consciousness, and I can imagine how panicked the dead man might have been, even if, by all appearances, he died in his sleep.

But the police findings came too late to commute P.'s eviction, and he did in fact go to live with the girl, for a few months, or maybe a year. By the time he told me this story, all of that was over. He didn't say much about how their relationship had ended; he was telling me the dead man's story. He didn't know what else I might hear in it, or why. I said I was sorry for his loss, and I showed it, too, by keeping quiet about my own experience of apnea and of the terror of not being able to reach out for help. You did what you could, I told him. You did what you could.

trial watchers

"Miss Martin, I know you're nervous, but please lean toward the microphone and speak as loudly and clearly as you can." The defense attorney tugs the bottom of his suit coat, seeming nervous himself—of the TV cameras, the prosecutor's many objections, the climate in this florescent-lit Florida courtroom. "Now, you were born in Terre Haute, Indiana, on September 12, 1980. Is that correct?"

"Yes," says Caitlin Martin, the defendant, the murderer. *Did you kill Brian Davis?* her lawyer had asked, moments ago. *Yes,* she'd whispered. The question and its answer were formalities. This trial isn't meant to determine Caitlin's guilt—we all know that she stabbed and then shot her lover, Brian Davis—but to classify her crime and determine a punishment. Those will be the jury's responsibilities. The rest of us here in the courtroom are under no obligation to be fair or impartial, and no one seems inclined to be. It's Friday, March 8: day twenty-four of the Caitlin Martin trial, day one of Caitlin's own testimony, and day five of five that my sister Jana and I will be here at the Orange County Courthouse, watching in person.

We began watching at home after Jana's surgery. She was treated for papillary thyroid cancer—a "good cancer," some dim-witted nurse told us, "especially in young women like you." "I'll pray for you," the same nurse had said, and Jana put her hand straight over my mouth. The cancer was "good" in that the growth would be easily excised, the errant cells scalded away with one dose of radioactive iodine. ("You'll still have your hair!" everyone congratulated her). But Jana had been practically quarantined, in the days after she drank her dose. Because of the radiation, no one was allowed to spend more than fifteen minutes at a time with her. She had to flush the toilet twice every time she used it. (And then what? Was there a separate septic system somewhere in the hospital, filtering her irradiated piss?) The magazines she brought with her, the body pillow, the half-knit scarf, would themselves have to be scanned before they could leave the ward. Relatively speaking, I'm sure all of that is "good." But it didn't feel good, to wave at my little sister from the other side of a thick window. She looked small and sickly in her cranked-up hospital bed, her dark hair lank, her eyes squeezed shut. Separated from her, both of us alone, I was more scared than I'd been since her diagnosis.

I would've liked someone to worry with but that wasn't how Jana wanted it. She didn't tell our parents about her illness, just as, three years before, she hadn't told them about her divorce until it was finalized. Mom and Dad are snowbirds now, wintering in Arizona; when they come home to Michigan this summer, she'll explain the scar at her throat as she'd explained her husband's absence: briefly, only after they ask. As then, she will leave out most of the details—to spare them unnecessary pain, she'll claim. But I know my parents will be hurt, again, that Jana didn't include them. Hurt that *we* excluded them from something so huge.

So it was just me with Jana, during and after her surgery—me and Caitlin Martin. "If you could volunteer to be on a jury, I would," Jana had whispered to me, from the other side of her sectional couch. She'd been released from the hospital just in time for opening arguments. On her big TV the chief prosecutor was waving his arms, and Jana's own hands hovered near the gauze bandage at her throat. She wanted to scratch her incision—we'd been working on that. Instead, she pressed her palms to the sides of her neck: "I can tell she's guilty by *looking* at her." Pressure made Jana's voice stronger. We'd thought back then (the doctors had said) that Jana would be speaking normally within a few weeks. Now, twenty-four days into the trial, it's clear that something happened to her vocal chords. The thyroid cancer message boards are full of dim prognoses about how long this side effect will last. Some of those posting used to be singers; they've lost whole octaves. Here's another bright side—Jana never could carry a tune—but I have the good sense not to point that out.

"What was life like for you," the defense attorney asks, "growing up in Terre Haute?"

"Good." Caitlin Martin speaks in a high, halting drawl. "When I was little, things were real good. My grandparents gave me a nice home. We lived way back in this pretty little holler . . . like something in a fairytale."

Her story sounds practiced but true, and as she describes her childhood, traces of another Caitlin play across her weary face—that fragile beauty I've seen in photos. I know Caitlin's backstory already, from the gossip magazines I bought during Jana's convalescence and from the tabloid TV shows we watched when the trial was off-air. I wasn't fascinated by the case the way my sister was, but after spending a full week of family sick-leave in front of Jana's TV, I was certainly well-acquainted with it. Like Jana, I know that Caitlin Martin had lived with her maternal grandparents until she was in eighth grade. That year, in the course of four months, her grandfather died and her grandmother developed Alzheimer's disease. I know that Caitlin's mother came back into the picture then, claiming to be clean, moving into the house in the holler to take care of Caitlin and the ailing grandmother. But, funded by Grandma's Social Security, Caitlin's mother was soon using again. For the next several years, Caitlin "pretty much was a nurse." She was held back in school; the bank took the house during her second freshman year. That's when relatives intervened to put Caitlin's grandmother in a nursing home. At sixteen, Caitlin was more than any of them could handle. She stayed with her mother when her mother had a place and otherwise she fended for herself.

"I was angry," she testifies. "Acting out. I hardly ever went to school and I had lots of boyfriends."

"What kind of boyfriends?" asks her lawyer. "Sometimes at that age people have hand-holding-type relationships, or 'boyfriends' who take them to dances. What were your relationships like?"

Caitlin glances at the jury, glances away. "Mostly sex."

"Try to speak clearly," her lawyer reminds her. "Now, you said they were mostly sexual? And what were the boys themselves like?"

"Older." Caitlin reddens. "Guys my mama knew."

"Did they treat you well?"

The prosecution objects to that phrasing; Caitlin's lawyer tries again: "Did the men you dated as a teenager ever abuse you, physically?"

Caitlin shrugs before remembering to say "Sometimes." Beside me, my sister writes quickly in her trial notebook. Jana's been writing about the trial from the beginning. Then, given the state of her vocal chords, it was easier for her to text me than to speak as we watched TV together. When her voice didn't come back, Jana extended her sick leave (she's an online marketing specialist, so she could work part-time from home). While she healed, she commented on the trial. She invented a new Twitter handle, a new blog—an entirely new persona for the occasion. "HatinCaitlinM" holds extreme views, but that's what it takes to gain entry into the "community" of trial-watchers... and the sentiment of Jana's handle isn't exaggerated. Whereas I see Caitlin as her lawyer wishes—as a victim of circumstance, pushed into the string of abusive relationships that she's now describing from the witness stand—Jana's seen her from the beginning as the villain painted by cable TV pundits. "An unnatural woman," proclaims Tamara Gold, host of *The Gold Standard.* Gold is ringleader of the court TV talking heads; with her Tammy Faye eyelashes, her platinum pompadour, and her stark delineations of good and evil, she's hardly *natural* herself. But her show relieves the burden of trial-watching for millions of viewers, who skip the protracted expert testimonies in favor of five-minute highlight reels and Gold's folksy judgments. By the Gold Standard, Caitlin is "guilty as a spark in a brushpile." Jana's commentary is often just as facile: "Accountability much? #Rememberthefallen #Justice-forBrian" or "Human tumor. #CaitlinMartin."

But there's no sense in my objecting to Jana's Tweets, not when I'm equally quick to accept Caitlin-as-victim. On the stand, prompted by her ponderous lawyer, Caitlin recounts dropping out of school at eighteen, in the fall of her junior year. She moved in with a forty-three-year-old man. "He was clean," she testifies. "That's all I cared about. He got drunk sometimes, but he didn't use—and he never, ever hit me." She managed to get her GED in the year she lived with him. And, because everyone had always told her she looked like Cinderella (she still does. Though her hair has dulled and her face thinned, she still has the bland features and big eyes of a Disney heroine), she formed an idea. "I always dreamt of being a princess—I mean actually working at Disney World." Her grandparents had taken her there for her tenth birthday, back when they were healthy and young. At nineteen, Caitlin took the bus from Terre Haute to Orlando.

I know the rest, too: Caitlin auditioned but wasn't cast as a Cinderella; she worked briefly in concessions at Disney but failed to master the park's extensive code of conduct. She'd been working odd jobs around Orlando for seven years by the time her temp agency sent her to Brian's realty firm. "He was so clean-cut and handsome," she says. "I didn't hardly know how to flirt with him." That hadn't mattered: "The first time he asked me to lunch we wound up back at his place."

Was this why I pitied her? I'd been a temp, fifteen years ago, living in Boston between college and library school. With my BA in English, I was a terrible typist, had no concept of filing, and had to be taught to operate a copier, a fax machine, a switchboard phone. I'd spent a year in a long-term placement, without insurance, vacation days, or respect from the be-suited lechers for whom I secretaried. When I was accepted to library school, I wept. It was that shocking to be valued again. This wasn't Caitlin's experience. When she left Brian's realty firm after four months, it was because she'd been fired, by him, for disconnecting too many client phone calls. Based on his feedback, the temp agency reassigned her to custodial work. Her relationship with Brian shifted, too.

"He never took me out anymore, except for fast food. He used to bring me flowers—my desk was up front, you know, so it was like decoration for the office. But he didn't do nice things after I got fired. And he told me all the time I was too dumb to be a secretary."

"Were those his words?"

She shakes her head. "He'd say I was too dumb to do anything but f—... the f-word."

"Miss Martin, will you say the phrase as Brian would, so it's clear to everyone?"

She fidgets, closing her eyes, then dives close to the microphone. "He'd say I was too dumb to do anything but fuck." Her consonants crack against the mic. "He'd say that all the time." She slumps back; her fair hair, now silvered, swings in front of her face. Caitlin is thirty-three, the same as Jana. If he were alive, Brian would be thirty-seven, like me.

The judge calls a twenty-minute recess. I tug my sister's arm so she'll stand for the jury's exit; she's that caught up in her notes. What details will the press have already shared with the world, live-blogging Caitlin's testimony from elsewhere in the courtroom? As a civilian, Jana isn't allowed to broadcast her reactions in-session. Still, she's gained credibility among the other trial-watchers for being here in person.

I was shocked when she decided to make the trip. At first I took her post as a re-Tweet: "Orlando bound! #MartinTrial #happiestplaceonearth." Maybe I should've said "What about your health?" or "Jana, that's disgusting"—but instead, I got her flight information and booked a ticket, too. I couldn't make Jana go alone into the company of rabid watchers like InjectCaitlin and Wild4Trialz. Now we've met these women, two matronly fifty-somethings; we've even eaten lunch with them (twice!)—but Jana doesn't waste any of today's short recess socializing. In the courthouse cafeteria she finds a seat and immediately begins typing on her tablet. I imagine remarks like "Another great performance from #CaitlinMartin #playingthevictim" and "Save a few tears for #BrianDavis #pityparty." My sister isn't a member of BriaNation, the online army that feverishly rebuts every courtroom questioning of Brian Davis's character. Though she advocates #JusticeforBrian, she's much more passionate about punishment for Caitlin.

"Why do you hate her so much?" I'd asked, back in the first days of the trial. We were sipping protein smoothies in front of Jana's television.

"I hate murderers," Jana had texted. "And her face is annoying."

On the TV screen, Caitlin sat doodling at the defense's table. The lawyers were arguing at sidebar and Jana's Twitter feed was going wild: how dare the accused appear bored? Caitlin had a heavy lower lip and a thin, unbowed upper lip—a perpetual pout, undisguised now by makeup. Despite appearances, I felt sympathetic toward her.

"She says it was self-defense."

"IF it was, she could've run away," texted Jana. "Or let him hit her—and then not gone back."

"Let him hit her?" My sister had been addled on painkillers.

"He's dead. Dead=worse than bruised," Jana texted. "She had choices."

"She was afraid for her life."

Jana shook her head, typing. "She said it happened before. IF that's true, she knew he wasn't going to kill her."

"Maybe that's not how it seemed, that night. Maybe it seemed like her only hope was to fight back. That's just instinct, isn't it, to fight back?"

Jana had looked at me then—not at the television, or her phone. The other side of the sectional seemed a long way away. The prosecutor resumed questioning the defense's witness and I thought Jana was going to ignore me. Then my phone buzzed. "No," she'd texted. After that, I had no more questions.

I was the one my sister called after she left Kyle, after she drove to a highway motel where she hoped he wouldn't look for her. I still lived in Boston, then, and that call was the first indication I'd had that anything was wrong. But as soon as she said he'd hit her, I felt like I should've known. At holidays, on vacations, I should've been paying closer attention—to Kyle's gestures, comments, attitudes—everything. I should've been there for Jana before she found herself in some cheap motel room. She was holed up in Michigan and I was a thousand miles away, snug in Massachusetts, where I'd lived for more than a decade.

"I'll fly you out here," I told her—I wanted her as far from Kyle as possible. She'd never had any distance from him, had dated him off and on through high school and then again after college, when they both moved back to our hometown. They got married at twenty-four. "Drive to the airport right now."

But she wouldn't budge, a cat caught up a tree. And so I went to her as quickly as I could. I stayed with her in that motel room over the weekend, holding her phone so she wouldn't take Kyle's calls (she asked me to do so, then begged each time to answer); I helped her find a new place to live. I went to their house while Kyle was at work and packed Jana's things. When I had to fly back East, after using up all my personal days at the Massachusetts Historical Society, I was hardly present in my own life. Kyle had abused her from the beginning, Jana finally confided.

"In high school?" I'd been away at college during those years, but I remembered my mother's concerns, shared over the phone: Jana was too serious about Kyle; she might be *sexually active.* I'd mocked those worries afterward, imitating my mother's nasal accent (an accent I'd only recently learned to hear) as I lay with my boyfriend in my narrow dorm bed.

"Since we got engaged . . ." Jana said. "Making the guest list . . . there was a mutual friend I didn't want to invite, because we hooked up once. And Kyle—was surprised by that, let's say. He was upset." "It's normal to be jealous," she'd argued, after I was back in Boston and she was on her own, moving between work and her new apartment, not telling her friends she'd split from Kyle, not talking to anyone except me. "I'm not *proud* I messed around with other people. I wish I hadn't."

I kept my phone on at all times back then, calling her from the closed stacks. Kyle knew where she lived, she mentioned. They'd had dinner a couple of times. She wasn't opposed to spending more time with him, she said. He seemed really lonely. I was visiting her as often as I could, leaving my cat under the care of successive friends, taking three-legged flights at odd times in order to afford airfare. When a position opened at the community college, back home, I applied. I was afraid not to. Staying at Jana's apartment for my interview— those three bare rooms, filled with only what I'd managed to pack, plus the cheap furniture we'd bought that first week—I couldn't tell whether she really lived there, or whether her life looked one way when I was there, and another when I was gone.

"Do you see him much?" I'd asked, the night after my interview. We were making dinner, realizing as we went along how many kitchen goods Jana had forfeited.

She shrugged. "A few times a week." She was chopping an onion with a steak knife.

"Do you see other people?" I watched her fingers, so close to the blade.

"What—now *you* think I'm a slut?" She chopped faster.

"No," I said. "What I meant was, do you see other people socially? And, Jana—I would *never* use that word."

"No?" She looked at me, resting her knife. "Not even if it was true?"

"*Slut* is a hypocritical misogynistic slur," I said. "You know that. Nobody who matters would think badly of you if you started dating again."

"I'm married—not divorced." Her eyes watered, though her fingers remained intact. "*Slut* is what *I'd* think. So drop it, Irene."

Maybe I should've dropped it for good—maybe I should've kept my distance and let her work it out according to her own timeframe and logic. But I'd seen the bruises around her right eye, down her neck. That first week, I'd watched them turn from purple to yellow—like how many other bruises I hadn't witnessed? I got the community college job, working at their library reference desk; I gave notice in Boston. Before I'd even unpacked in Michigan, I took Jana to see a divorce lawyer. That first appointment was just a conversation, explaining the process—but the lawyer followed up and I followed up even more persistently. I pestered her, really, and finally she filed. I helped Jana to correct an unfortunate misstep. Caitlin Martin hadn't had a sister or even any close friends. She had only her own hopes that Brian would change, the bouquets would return, the abuses stop. *Look what happened,* I had to stop myself from telling Jana, every time we watched the trial. *Look what I spared you from.*

Caitlin's attorney approaches her again, more rumpled after the recess. He can't have been sleeping, though his clothes suggest otherwise, his crooked comb-over. He clears his throat wetly. "Miss Martin, in the months leading up to December 11, 2008, did you and Mr. Davis have any other notable fights?"

The prosecution objects to the word "fight"—they contend that Brian was taken unawares on the night of his death—and Caitlin's attorney rephrases: "Did Mr. Davis use physical force against you in the months leading up to December 11, 2008?"

Caitlin nods. "This one time, probably in October, he let me borrow his car. I was supposed to fill it up afterward but I didn't have enough money, so I got just a couple of gallons. More than I used—but Brian got real mad. I hadn't 'respected our agreement,' he said. He grabbed my arm and threw me down, right on his driveway. It still hurts sometimes." She rubs her bicep.

"Did you see a doctor?"

"I couldn't afford that."

"So nothing went on record. Were there other physical incidents?"

"Yessir. He got real upset whenever I messed with his stuff. Like, if I put wooden spoons in the dishwasher or used the wrong sponge on the counter. He'd make me pay for those things."

"What did that mean—'pay'?"

She shakes her head, biting her fat lower lip. "He'd always say I wasn't worth much—I only made $12 an hour with the temp agency. Less than a whore, he'd say. So if I did something wrong he'd decide how much it was worth, and I'd have to do—things—until I paid him back. Sex things."

"But you had a consensual sexual relationship—this was a game?"

She closes her eyes. "I wasn't supposed to say no."

"Did you enjoy this arrangement?"

She shakes her head, then remembers—"No."

"And did you have sexual relations, outside of this system?"

"Not really." Caitlin pulls a tissue from the box on the witness stand. "I was always doing something wrong."

"Miss Martin, why did you stay in this relationship?"

I look at Jana, writing steadily. She's fashioned a narrow French braid across her hairline, pinning it behind her left ear. It's a hairstyle we've admired on models, in magazines—something I'd never have the dexterity to do, even if my hair was long enough. With her hair pulled back, I can see my sister's expression, intent on the proceedings but unchanged by that question.

"I loved him," Caitlin says. Her Disney eyes widen, as though she's surprised that this, at least, isn't obvious.

"Did you believe that he loved you?"

"Oh, no." Caitlin shakes her head. "I wished—but I wasn't in his league. I only figured he might stay with me if I did what he said to."

Now my sister rolls her eyes. It is disgusting—the whole truth, or this scripted version of it.

"Did you feel that being with him, even under the circumstances, was better than not being with him?"

"Yessir. He was the first person I'd known in a long time that had goals. He was—thinking about the future." Her voice breaks.

"Miss Martin, are you ready to talk about the night of December 11, 2008?"

"Yes," she whispers. "I can talk about it."

HE CAN'T, my sister scrawls. #JusticeforBrian, I supply, reflexively. The whole truth is that I'm not sorry he's dead, that smirking blond salesman from the evidence photos, broad and fit and tan. It's easy to imagine him talking clients into more expensive homes than they can afford; easy to imagine him intimidating a damaged person like Caitlin. He was popular in high school, his friends have told the gossip magazines. As if that's a virtue.

When Jana divorced Kyle, her lawyer suggested filing a restraining order. It was standard practice, the lawyer said, used to demonstrate irreconcilable differences. I was surprised to learn how easy it was to get a restraining order. Just ask, just offer a reason that you don't want someone near you, and the court will make that reason official. The order isn't enforced, of course, unless the person holding it contacts the police. So for Jana to have this thing on record didn't really mean much, as I tried to persuade her. Still, she couldn't fathom "doing that to Kyle." I don't know whether she told him that this idea had been proposed and that I was behind it; I don't know *what* she told him, about me or anything else. But when, for two weeks straight, I was followed home from work by a black Dodge Charger, I filed a restraining order against him, myself. After that, as long as I was near Jana, Kyle couldn't be. He knew this, having received notice of the order; my sister knew it, too.

Naturally our parents were confused by my sudden move back to Michigan. They'd enjoyed visiting me in Boston, walking the Freedom Trail and wandering Mount Auburn Cemetery. My life there fit their idea of me as the bookish daughter, become a librarian in a craggy, quaint city. I couldn't betray Jana by telling them the whole truth, so I told them something else—that I was ready for a change, wanted to be near my sister, missed Lake Michigan. All of which was true. I didn't tell them about Kyle, and I didn't tell them the other thing: that it was exciting to let go of my Boston life and its routines—to just let go of what had grown familiar. It felt freeing, at first, as though I could become someone new and help my sister transform, in the process.

But we neither transformed nor reverted to the easy companionship of our childhood. It was hard being around Jana during and after the divorce. She was sullen or frantic, rarely engaged by our conversations and activities. And I hadn't given enough thought to what my choices would mean between me and my parents. When, that Christmas three years ago, Jana had explained that she and Kyle were separated, my mother turned to me. She didn't say anything, but her feelings were there on her face, her recognition of what I'd kept secret. My parents had always encouraged the two of us to stick up for each other, but it was clear from my mother's glance that this wasn't where she'd expected that loyalty to lead. "You could've come to us," my mother said. "You should have." She hugged Jana but looked at me. "Honey, I'm sorry."

If anyone actually started over, after the divorce, it was Kyle. For a few months following the proceedings, he continued to haunt us—a gleaming black shadow far in my rearview mirror; a spate of weepy messages on Jana's voicemail. The few friends I'd reconnected with in our hometown passed along stories: he hooked up with a twenty-year-old, got thrown out of a bar downtown. We didn't fact-check these rumors. Or maybe Jana did, maybe she was still seeing him sometimes—I can't say for sure. But the summer after the split, Kyle left town. He moved to Colorado, we heard; all Jana knew was that she woke up one morning to a call from her building manager. Some guy had left a bunch of boxes for her, and could she move them out of the lobby ASAP? When she opened them, she found that Kyle had packed up every item from their wedding registry. Some things were unused, others well-worn. Kyle loved her, Jana insisted, but he'd relinquished everything that represented their six-year marriage. I was glad these boxes had been left without a note, in a humble rather than grand gesture. Kyle was gone; my sister could start over. That very afternoon she bought her giant beige sectional and a queen-sized bed.

When court adjourns for the day—our final day in Orlando—we've heard Caitlin's description of the events of December 11, 2008. She'd tried and failed to turn on Brian's bedroom television.

"He kept screaming about the receiver," she testified, "but there was no 'receiver' button on the clicker." She'd attempted to turn the components on manually. But "Do it right!" he'd yelled. He threw the remotes at her, striking her on the temple with one, nicking the drywall with another. "That made him mad," she testified. He didn't care that he'd hurt her, only that he'd hurt the house. "You're going to pay for that," he'd shouted—and for once, she said no. She ran from the room but he ran faster, blocking the front door. "Where are you going?" he'd taunted. "You've got work to do, girl." He'd taken her purse, her phone, holding them out of reach. She tried the landline. Caitlin described Brian laughing at her—the phone wasn't hooked up.

"He said I still didn't know how to use a phone. He said firing me was the best choice he'd ever made. I remember him taking off his belt." On the witness stand she stopped, shaking her head.

"Then what happened?"

"I don't know!" She said it straight to the jury, speaking loudly for once. "I don't remember!" *Selective amnesia*, my sister wrote on her notepad. But Caitlin seemed genuinely agitated as she described the next thing she remembered: being in Brian's car—and seeing her own bloody reflection in the rearview mirror. "There was something..." She waved her hand across her face.

"I went back inside," she said, "to wash up. I didn't know... And then I saw something on the carpeting—this big red stripe, like something got drug down the hall."

"When you saw that, what did you do?"

"I yelled for Brian," she said. "I couldn't find my phone to call for help."

Caitlin recounted following that trail, to find Brian on the floor of his bedroom, face-down.

"I went over to him, and when I came up by his waist, he grabbed my ankle—like in a scary movie. His hand . . . was all red. And he said—it was awful—he said 'I'm going to kill you, you retarded bitch.' And he jerked real hard on my ankle, and I fell against the dresser and hit my head—right where he'd gotten me with the clicker."

That's when Caitlin remembered the loaded gun Brian kept in his sock drawer. Something he bragged about, she said (and I could only imagine how BriaNation would react; Brian was surely responsible in gun ownership as in everything else). Her head was throbbing and Brian was still coming after her, dragging himself along the floor. She took the gun from the drawer.

"Did he see it?"

"I think so, because he came at me faster."

"Still crawling?"

"Yes."

"And you didn't run?"

"I would've had to jump over him, and he'd already pulled me down once."

"So what did you do?"

"I fired the gun."

"Were you trying to shoot him?"

"I was trying to scare him."

"You weren't aiming the gun at Brian when you fired?"

"I didn't know how to use it—I'd never even held a gun before."

"Do you remember hitting him?"

"No."

"Do you remember shooting the gun again?"

"No."

She shot him six times, as we all knew. As she described

it, Brian Davis's family members wept and embraced in the front row of the gallery. Were they imagining Brian's pain, or how he'd treated Caitlin? The cable station's big HD camera swiveled toward the family and Jana adjusted the scarf at her throat.

"Miss Martin," said the attorney, "do you remember what happened next?"

She shook her head. "I must've walked home."

A twelve-mile walk with blood on her face in the middle of the night. Did someone pick her up from Brian's? She couldn't remember. Nor did she remember what she'd done with the gun; she couldn't remember anything about the knife. But it's impossible, or nearly so, that anyone *but* Caitlin disposed of those weapons. They were found, wiped, in a brackish lake behind a discount shopping center, just across the highway from her apartment complex. Caitlin lived in Pine Hills, a rough part of Orlando—dangerous enough for Tamara Gold to ask, "What was a 'nice' girl like her doing in Crime Hills?" Did Caitlin assume, when she dumped her weapons, that they'd just blend in with all the others? Instead, they were found within forty-eight hours of Brian's death. A partial print was taken from the handle of the 8-inch chef's knife—the only piece missing from Brian's Wüsthof set. The shopping center even turned over fuzzy surveillance footage of a slim figure crossing the parking lot on December 12. In other words, Caitlin had no idea how not to get caught.

On the stand, she clutched a tissue, weeping or pretending to. *She only cries for herself,* Jana wrote. *Never for Brian.* But I can bring myself to the verge of panic by imagining myself in Caitlin's place, that night or in the witness box. In Caitlin's place, I would've done anything to save myself.

When court adjourns for the day, Jana and I file outside. We won't be back, thank God. We will soon become rational creatures again, interested in matters of consequence. Even so, I offer to take a picture of Jana in front of the courthouse—a souvenir.

"Sure," she whispers. She re-ties her scarf, eyeing the varied crowd on the plaza. Every day we leave the orderly courtroom to meet BriaNation in full regalia. Supporters of the Davis family carry homemade signs and distribute buttons; Brian's face is everywhere. On Wednesday, a trial-watcher was even arrested for trying too insistently to hug a grieving Davis. Cable crews troll this motley crowd, angling for interviews. It's a scene we'll remember, with or without photographs. Still, I dig through my tote for my camera.

When I look up, my sister is waving to someone. CaitlinMartian, TrialWatcher69, Wild4Trialz—all of Jana's friends know that we're flying home tomorrow, all will want to say goodbye. But approaching us, quickly, is a woman with tall yellow hair, an electric blue powersuit. A familiar face—but not, I realize, from among our circle of courtroom acquaintances. It's Tamara Gold, of *The Gold Standard.*

Jana waves again and Gold calls out: "Which of ya'll girls is the blogger?" My camera is in my hands; I raise it, take the incredible picture of my sister shaking hands with Gold, then being led away by a waifish young man with gelled hair and a clipboard. The portion of BriaNation that orbits the cable crews closes around Gold and Jana, trundling in a mass toward a more scenic corner of the plaza. They leave me behind. Jana is right there, I know, but from this vantage, I can't be sure that she hasn't disappeared.

Which one of you is the blogger?—I find my phone at the bottom of my bag, turn it on. "Domestic violence is a cancer," Jana had Tweeted earlier, "Remember the real victim #EarlyDetection #Survivor #JusticeforBrian." The post links back to her blog—to the post she wrote at recess:

As a cancer survivor, I know what it's like to be surprised. By the time I knew my thyroid was diseased, the only way to save myself was to get rid of it. That's the situation that Brian was in. Caitlin Martin was a cancer, but he couldn't see it, no matter how hard he looked. He couldn't see she had changed from normal to malignant. We don't know exactly why that happened—whether Caitlin mutated or was cancerous from birth—but we do know that Brian should have gotten rid of her at the first sign of abnormality. He was too trusting to do this, and because of his kindness he made the ultimate sacrifice.

I read it again, lingering on that last phrase. *The ultimate sacrifice?* If Jana were beside me, instead of lost inside that sycophantic circle, I'd ask her how she could use such language—this trite, militaristic euphemism—to describe being killed in a domestic dispute. Sacrifice denotes willingness, I'd tell her; sacrifice means giving up something *for* someone else.

But what would my protest mean, when many, many trial-watchers have already reposted this paragraph of Jana's? I scroll through dozens of supportive notes in her comments section. This is no place for me to post my objections. If I un-followed her now, HatinCaitlinM wouldn't even notice.

I wait for nearly an hour on the plaza—watching the crowd thin and skateboarders emerge, to grind down the concrete stairs—before Gold's assistant finds me.

"Miss Karlin? Your sister asked me to tell you that you should meet her back at the hotel."

"No," I say, reflexively. "How will she get there without me?"
Miss Gold will take care of that, he assures me; it won't
be much longer.

"My sister can barely speak—I don't understand how an
interview, or whatever they're doing, could take this long."

"Everyone is aware of Mrs. Sheehan's condition. Miss
Gold's production team just has a few details left to work
out with your sister."

Mrs. Sheehan—Jana's married name, her legal name.
It's as unexpected as the phrase *production team.* "Is Jana
going to be on TV?" I've never seen anything approaching
this fuss when the cable crew solicits reactions on the plaza.
But I've never paid much attention, either.

"I'm not at liberty, but I'm sure Mrs. Sheehan will
explain everything later."

"I'd rather wait here."

"Miss Karlin, your sister left with Miss Gold. The easiest
thing would be to wait for her at the hotel. Miss Gold's driver
will deliver Mrs. Sheehan in just a bit, safe and sound."

I check my phone. Its blankness confirms what he's
saying: Jana has abandoned me. And so I go.

Alone in our musty hotel room, I find the court
channel, but I can't bear to listen to it, or even to watch
its muted faces, frowning earnestly. I pack my suitcase,
pack Jana's, too, ticking off the minutes until our flight
the next morning. I'm glad we didn't allow an extra day
for Universal Studios, Gatorland, Disney World—any of
the garish amusements whose brochures litter this cheap
room. Jana spent her honeymoon at Disney, but I've never
been; our family never made that trip. In fact I've only
visited Florida once before this, over the Labor Day
weekend following my college graduation. My senior-year
boyfriend had been recruited by a consulting firm; he was
rooming with another new consultant, in an apartment

paid for by the firm. He drove a company car and had already identified the company girl he would date after me. The attraction we'd felt for each other at college, tucked away in the mountains of western Massachusetts, didn't translate into the denuded landscape of central Florida. I remember the stark white beaches, the bleached-white sky, the sheen of sweat and oil on my clammy white face. I felt incongruous and plain at beachside bars; I felt shy of the body he'd built over the summer, working out to kill time until his job started.

That relationship amounted to nothing; he's someone I sometimes forget, when I tally the men I've been with. But being in Florida for the trial reminds me of who I was, on that other visit—someone awkward and confused, a stranger even to the calendar of my post-college life. That boyfriend dumped me on the drive to the Tampa airport, and as soon as I landed in Boston, I began my stint as a temp. Now, fifteen years later I'm waiting in an Orlando hotel room for my sister, on the eve of flying back to our hometown. I could almost believe that my life away from her never happened, or mattered.

I tap my phone to life: no messages. But at the top of my meager Twitter feed—

"Meet your new on-air correspondent! @GoldStandard #JusticeforBrian."

I'm still considering this when the card reader buzzes and Jana comes in. She waves, an exhausted gesture. It's almost ten o'clock. We've gotten up every morning this week at four to get seats in the gallery. Ten o'clock in a strange town, and Jana didn't message me about her whereabouts—except insofar as she Tweeted her followers. Now she nods to my phone.

"You saw?" she asks aloud.

"I did."

"No congratulations?" Her hand goes to her throat and she pulls her phone from her blazer pocket. "Did you watch my segment?" she texts.

"I missed it."

"They'll be more," she types. "They hired me as a commentator!"

"You can't speak." It's the first thing that comes to my mind. *How could you?* is next.

"I'll type," she texts. "Like this, but on-air with Tamara. They'll have a display on half the screen. It's a new angle."

"Jana . . . You want to be part of this?"

She blinks at me. "Why do you think I came down here?" she texts.

"To get a spot on *The Gold Standard*?"

"What—you're above this kind of thing? :P"

Yes, I'd like to answer—but after all, I'm here. "This is going to affect your life, Jana. Your job."

She waves her hand, then types: "This IS my job now. This is something I care about."

"What will Mom and Dad think?" This is how they'll find out she's had cancer . . . by seeing her on court TV, an expert trial-watcher with a sad backstory.

"They'll be proud." She takes off her blazer, hangs it carefully. She's right; that's how our parents will *say* they feel.

"Jana . . . you realize that Kyle will see you?"

She shrugs, her back to me. She unzips her suitcase and begins unfolding the clothes I just packed. Jana's being on TV will be big news back home. Kyle's parents will be sure to tell him. From there, no doubt he'll find Jana's blog, her zealous condemnations of Caitlin.

"That boy with the clipboard called you Mrs. Sheehan."

She reaches again for her phone. "It's my name," she texts.

"But when Kyle sees that on TV, what does it say? It says you're still his."

"That's your opinion."

"Don't you think he'll get in touch with you?" He'll be upset that she's suffered without him. He won't be able to handle her not needing him. "Jana—you're not doing this to get him back—are you?"

She turns to face me, shaking her head. "Go to hell," she rasps.

"Why, then? Why would you want to be a lackey for some über-conservative witch?"

"That's your *opinion*," she says, then types. "Thirty-four. Divorced. Cancer. Not going to waste more time."

"I can understand wanting a change; that's natural after trauma. But *this*?"

"A once-in-a-lifetime opportunity. A chance to make a difference."

Clichés—but to point that out would be pointless. "You could do that in so many ways. With your skill set, if we moved out East, you could do anything you wanted."

"Your world, not mine."

"So Seattle, then, San Francisco. We'll go together, start over."

"Start. Over." she types. "Get it?"

"Why would you want to add to this *spectacle*? It's gross, Jana, it's not you. We could go anywhere, do anything. "

"No," Jana says aloud, "*we* can't." Her weakened voice is almost a sigh. "Irene—how can I start over if you're with me?"

Suddenly she appears beside herself on the muted TV. That other Jana smiles at the camera, tilting her head toward Gold's foam-tipped microphone. What's she saying?

"I need space," Jana texts. "I need to do my own thing." She clears her throat. "I'm sorry," she says.

"It's not you, it's me," I say. "Didn't you forget that one?"

"Irene—stop. I want this. They want me. Why can't you *ever* be happy for me?" The living Jana frowns beside her doppelgänger.

"I can't be happy when you're making a terrible decision."
She opens her mouth, then winces, texts. "I'm staying
until the trial's over. After that, we'll see."

"Jana, I—" What? *I don't want you to treat me like this?*
I moved to Michigan for you, so you can't do this to me? I
try again: "You're better than this."

"This is a good thing," she texts. "An opportunity. You &
I will be happier living our own lives again."

I think of what my résumé will look like, the cover letter
that will be necessary to explain my choices. What's left of
my own life?

"You could move in with Mom & Dad," she types. "Until
you figure out what you want."

She's serious, and I feel my throat closing as it does when
I'm angry. I've always cried when I want to scream, always
looked weaker than I am. I walked willingly into all of this—
sacrificing my life and career to "save" my sister, who maybe
only needed a scapegoat. Someone to seem like the
instigator, the villain, the author of restraining orders.
Someone to take care of her until she was recovered. If she
ever needed me at all.

"I could slap you." I know full well what I'm saying.

Her dark eyes widen. "No," she says. "You could not."

I shake my head to push back the pain in my throat; I
can barely speak. I take up my phone: "I love you," I text
her. "I'm here if you need me."

"Oh, Reny," Jana's sharp features go soft. She crosses
the room, hugs me—so close that I can feel her scarf against
my neck. "I know. And I couldn't have done this without
you. I really couldn't."

The Martin trial will go on for weeks and weeks, and my
sister will weigh in on each day's proceedings. On air, her
hair will grow higher and glossier, her outfits a succession

of primary colors. Always, her blouses will fall open at the throat, displaying a scar lightened by makeup but still insistent. Jana will smile silently as Tamara Gold inveighs against "the new Delilah," then she'll offer a more restrained version of the same sentiment: "Caitlin simply doesn't value human life."

When her voice is up to it, Jana will call me on weekends. I won't know, I won't ask, what her life in Florida consists of, besides *The Gold Standard.* I won't follow the trial itself anymore, though I'll know where it's heading. Instead I'll send out job applications, make amends with my parents, focus on my new beginning.

Eventually, late some night, I'll seek out Jana's first interview with Tamara Gold. I know that in it, Jana will still look like herself, with her braided crown of hair and a creamy scarf to hide her scar. She'll press her palms to her neck, then lower her hands before leaning close to the microphone. "This case has inspired a passion in me," she'll say. Her voice will sound clear and strong, with what effort only I know. "I hope to draw attention to it through my blog; I hope I can be a small part of justice for Brian and others like him." And Tamara Gold, hugging my sister with one arm, will say "You are so brave, to come down here in your condition. To sacrifice so much, for a total stranger."

lost boy not found

The FBI releases its test results to *all concerned parties.*
These include: the Detroit papers, the New York papers,
the television news programs, the man, the man's supposed
family, and the family his DNA has denied. He *could not
have shared a mother* with the sister he would claim. His
other sister, his supposed half-sister, is quoted widely. *He
lost two families today,* she says. *He's always saying
something.* It is a matter of record that the two of them
don't share a mother, either.

The man does not return now to the local library, does
not leave his *modest single-story home.* He does not open
his door to the reporters and photographers who loved him
just last week. Then, they'd asked him to cock his head—
as the lost boy does in black-and-white snapshots. They'd
marveled over the likeness and taken quotes. Always, he
told the reporters, he's suspected that he *came from other
people.* Always he's felt *different from the rest* of his
supposed family. For years he scoured sleuth sites and
ancestry boards, looking for his other life, his real age and
name. And then: a birthmark on a missing boy's calf, a scar
on his chin. The man had trembled, tracing these on his

own body—features *last seen on October 31, 1955.* He has the other father's round face, the other mother's deep-set eyes. He has, eventually, a swab from the true sister's mouth. This sister, his sister, is listed by her maiden name in an Iowa phone book, as if she's been waiting there for his call. Amazing how the years have scattered them! The last time he saw her, outside of memory, she was an infant in a stroller on a Long Island sidewalk. He can't remember how the kidnappers lured him away from her. He can't remember why he stepped out of his rightful life, or how he stepped into this one. But the home DNA kit proved what he and she both had felt, that day on the phone: they might be related.

Were his false parents behind the kidnapping? He gave the reporters *no comment.* His "parents" are long divorced; his "mother" *could not be reached.* But his false father spoke to the papers at length: *That boy was right here beside me* in October, 1955. That boy was *never out of my sight.* How can this be true, when, in all the years since, they have never been close? Let the tests say what they will, let the papers print what they want—but if he isn't the missing boy, who is? Why not let that boy be found? Think of the sister in Iowa—think of what she's lived with these fifty-odd years. He could be her brother, now. He could tear up his faked birth certificate and become himself again.

The lost man sits in his yard with his dog and wishes away the publicity that makes it impossible for him to be family to anyone now. Just down the road his supposed father is thinking hard thoughts against him, while in Iowa the phone rings and rings. He imagines a woman with eyes like his looking out over a flatter yard. It's earlier, there. Here, his wife leaves their phone off the hook and all day strange cars drive slowly past. What do they want from him? Disproved, the man has become *an unemployed laborer who lives with his wife, 195 miles northwest of Detroit.* But the facts haven't changed. The man is a boy who went missing a long, long time ago—and there for a minute, the world came looking for him.

Acknowledgments

These stories were written and published over the course of many years. Thank you to my teachers and classmates at Syracuse University and the University of Missouri for insights and inspiration. Thank you to more recent readers Michael Piafsky, Robert Long Foreman, Mika Yamamoto, and Katie Curnow for feedback and encouragement.

I am very grateful to all of the editors who've published these stories, but particularly to the brilliant Heather Jacobs at *Big Fiction*, for helping me to understand what was missing and what was in excess.

For the gifts of concentration and community, many thanks to the Hambidge Center for Creative Arts and Sciences, Kimmel Harding Nelson Center, Artsmith, Ragdale, Talemor Park, and Dickinson House. Special thanks to the women of Hambidge, Summer 2014, whose examples and wisdom helped me to reorient myself toward my work.

Thank you to Éireann Lorsung for creating the sanctuary of Dickinson House and for sharing more of your magic with me through this book's cover design.

Thank you to Press 53's Kevin Morgan Watson for selecting my manuscript and tending to it with patience and care.

Thank you to my wonderful family—to my father, who might appear as a character in one of these stories, and to my mother and sister, who definitely do not.

And thank you to my partner Tim, for love and support, for reading all of this and for helping in so many ways.

Stephanie Carpenter was born and raised in Traverse City, Michigan. She holds an MFA from Syracuse University and a PhD in English and Creative Writing from the University of Missouri. Her current project, a pair of novellas about professional female artists in nineteenth-century New England, has received fellowships from the American Antiquarian Society, the Sewanee Writers' Conference, and the Winterthur Museum, Garden and Library. She currently teaches creative writing and literature at Michigan Tech University, in the northernmost reaches of Michigan's Upper Peninsula.